Merry X mas to you
arthur

Aunt Florence

Prince
Godfrey

Prince Godfrey

THE KNIGHT OF THE
STAR OF THE NATIVITY

*Twelve Wondrous Tales Recorded by
Master Johannes Sarabandus, His
Majesty's Astrologer.*

Halina Gorska

Introduction by Phyllis Fenner

Illuminated by Irena Lorentowicz

ROY PUBLISHERS   NEW YORK

Printed in the United States of America
Kingsport Press, Kingsport, Tenn.

Foreword

I T is not given to most of us to speak many languages, nor can most of us travel far. But we can read books from other countries, and books are, in a way, a common language, one we all can understand. The Pinnochios, the Heidis, the Babars, the Mary Poppins, the folktales and legends we love, bring us closer to the countries from which they come. They show us the things the people of those countries laugh at, the things they fear, the things they love, the things they believe. And when people love and understand the same things they are more likely to love each other.

Within this lovely book are twelve wondrous tales concerning Prince Godfrey. They will remind you of King Arthur and his Knights of the Round Table in the gallant adventures and miraculous happenings, and in the beauty and dignity with which they are written. They are the adventures of one brave knight who was like Sir Galahad in his purity and kindliness. He was also a bard, and sometimes defeated his enemy with a song. The story is told by the astrologer of his father's court, who prophesied what was to come. "There is nothing so strange that it might not come to pass in the world."

A writer for children must have something more than a gift for writing. She must have a deep feeling for childhood and a very warm heart. Surely, Halina Gorska, who wrote this book, had these in abundance. All gifts seemed to be hers: wealth, beauty, and opportunity. She was intensely interested in people. It seemed to her that there were no bad people. All people were good if they only believed in themselves. She wondered why men differed, and why it was so difficult for people to realize the simple idea of a world brotherhood. It seemed so clear to her that we were here to help each other.

What Halina Gorska believed she put into practice in her own living. At seventeen she started a club for poor boys and girls in Warsaw. Later she wrote a book about her work in which she told of some of the problems of these children. When she married and moved to Lwow she kept her interest in these children, and one cold winter she opened a clubhouse for newsboys. By her work, her books, and her radio programs, she interested others in what she was doing.

Halina Gorska is no more, but her spirit lives in the things she wrote and in the memories of the people who knew her. When you have read this book, "Prince Godfrey," you, too, will know something of the beauty of her spirit, and that of the country from which she came.

PHYLLIS FENNER

Contents

While still a tender child he shall be bereaved of his parents in the turmoil of war.

From the prison where he shall be confined by a kinsman and guardian, he shall
be delivered by birds, and shall cross the
sea on their wings.

In a strange, far-off land, clad not in silk
or velvet, but in sackcloth, he shall tend
sheep.

Lured by elves, he shall be saved from
dire danger by the miraculous power of
his songs.

He shall free mountain dwellers and little
shepherds from a savage werewolf and
from witches.

Introduction

O N Christmas Eve, in the year of our Lord [here the manuscript is illegible], crowds overran the courtyard of the castle. All eyes were fixed on the parapet whence the herald was to proclaim the great tidings. All hearts beat in unison praying the Lord for one thing. Never had an heir been more fervently awaited by the people. And no wonder. The king's brother, Prince Gerald, who would have succeeded to the throne, had the king remained childless, was known for his cruel, treacherous and violent character. It was difficult indeed to tell if he was feared more than he was hated. Yet a strange anxiety gripped everybody, for it seemed as if, through peculiar signs, God wished to announce the coming of extraordinary events. That a thunderstorm should occur in December was truly something unheard-of; and yet, two days before Christmas Eve, a tempest broke with such fury that the day was black with clouds and the night was bright with lightning, and trees toppled in the wind. For two days and two nights the storm raged, until on the third day, just on Christmas Eve, it suddenly blew over. The sky cleared, the sun shone as if it were March or even April, and the air was as warm and fragrant as it is in May.

Dusk had fallen, but no one moved to go home for the evening meal. And then, at the very moment when the first star flashed in the sky, the same star that had long ago guided the shepherds in Bethlehem, two servants bearing torches appeared on the parapet, followed by the king's herald.

"Long live the son and heir of our lord," burst in a mighty clamor from a thousand throats. But suddenly all was still as the multitude beheld something unusual; overhead, in a silvery, blinding brilliance, appeared a snow-white dove, followed by a black hawk.

At lightning speed the dove circled over the courtyard and entered the castle through an open window above the head of the herald, with the cruel hawk pursuing it. The dove winged through one hall after another and, when it came to the chamber where the queen lay, dropped with its last strength on the breast of the little prince sleeping in the cradle.

The hawk was about to pounce upon the dove, meaning to snatch it away, but suddenly, as if frightened by the infant, it recoiled with a fearful shriek, struck its head on a lyre that hung on the wall, and fell to the ground, dead.

Greatly alarmed, the king summoned me and spoke this:

"You have witnessed all the strange signs which attended the birth of my son and heir. Tell me, master, what they mean and what the future has in store for my son."

"Gracious king," said I, "give me three days, that I may turn to my books and the stars for help, and I shall comply with your wish."

"Be it so, though my heart trembles with anxiety and impatience," replied the king. "I command all my knights to be in attendance in the throne room three days hence. In the midst of my faithful vassals, I shall hear your answer. Take care, however, to relate only what you will have learned from the books and the stars, adding nought to reassure or flatter me."

When three days later I was summoned to face the king, I found my gracious lord on the throne, surrounded by all his vassals. At his right stood Prince Gerald, gloomy and sullen as usual, his hand resting on the hilt of his sword, and on purple-covered benches along the walls were seated illustrious earls and barons.

I bowed deeply to the king and spoke these words:

"My king, and noble sirs, this is the prediction which I have read in the stars and the books. Prince Godfrey the Conqueror (for so he shall be known by all) was born under the miraculous and mysterious sign of the Star of the Nativity. He shall become the greatest knight and bard that has existed or shall exist in all Christendom, and on the night of Christmas he shall be endowed with superhuman might which shall give him victory over every power. He is predestined to a life full of danger and glory, and these twelve wonders shall come to pass:

"While still a tender child he shall be bereaved of his parents in the turmoil of war.

"From the prison where he shall be confined by a kinsman and guardian, he shall be delivered by birds, and shall cross the sea on their wings.

"In a strange, far-off land, clad not in silk or velvet, but in sackcloth, he shall tend sheep.

"Lured by elves, he shall be saved from dire danger by the miraculous power of his songs.

"He shall free mountain dwellers and little shepherds from a savage werewolf and from witches.

"He shall heal the daughter of a mighty king, and shall be made a page at the king's court.

"Having defeated the conqueror of a hundred tourneys, he shall win his knight's spurs.

"Without drawing his sword, he shall capture a castle which the king himself and his whole army would not have dared to attempt.

"The Princess of the Seas shall present him with a magic ring that shall give him power over the ocean.

"Vivian the Sorceress shall bestow upon him an amethyst of miraculous and mysterious power.

"Upon his return to his own land, he shall drive out the tyrant who shall have seized his throne, and he shall rule long and happily ever after.

"He shall deliver the fairest princess on earth from the captivity of a ruler who knocks down mountains at a single stroke.

"And so I have told you all that I have read in the

books and in the stars, adding nothing to set your heart at rest, sire, or to flatter you."

Starting up with great fury Prince Gerald advanced a few steps toward me, and spoke threateningly:

"Crafty old man. What have I done to you that you wish to turn my brother against me? Truly, but for my deference to his majesty, I should draw my sword and slay you here and now like a dog. Why, it is common knowledge that the king has no kin other than myself; thus it is of me you speak, knave, when you say that I shall keep my beloved nephew imprisoned. You lying cheat!"

"I am but an astrologer," I replied, "and I am duty bound to proclaim what I read in the stars, with nothing added or withheld. Therefore be silent, prince, for your words are highly insulting."

The king knitted his brow.

"You must take me for a doddering old man or a senseless child," he said, "a child that will believe any tale, be it of crossing seas on wings, of a ruler who tumbles mountains, or of a knight who vanquishes foes without a sword. Were it not for your white hair, your fraudulent inventions would not go unpunished, the more so since you dare cast discredit upon the honor of my brother."

"Do you speak thus to me, my king," I inquired, "to me whom you were wont to call a friend? Since when, sire, do you regard me as a liar? True, my predictions sound strange today; but there is nothing so strange that it might not come to pass. How can you know that your son will not cross the sea on wings, or will not defeat his enemies with his song, if it may so please the Lord? How can you tell that there is no ruler who knocks down mountains at a single stroke? Have you visited all lands and seas and valleys and mountains? Have you penetrated into the earth and viewed the upper spheres? And had you done so and found no such man, may he not at any moment arise in the world if it should so please the Master of Heaven?"

But the king would not hearken to me, and dismissed me with a wave of the hand. Away, then, I went, with sadness in my heart. From then on I lost my master's trust, but the future, as this book shall reveal, proved all my prophecies to be true.

Yet not in praise of my own wisdom did I write it,

but in order to make secure the fame of the science which I serve. And mind, I do not here recount the whole life of Prince Godfrey, the famed knight, for I should have to write twelve books, and not twelve tales, concerning his remarkable deeds, but merely that part of his life which has to do with my predictions.

Tale 1

C *While still a tender child he shall be bereaved of his parents in the turmoil of war.*

THERE was no end to the gracious king's rejoicing in his son. He could not feast his eyes enough on him, and he knew not himself how to thank God for the child.

Beautiful, indeed, was little Prince Godfrey. When sometimes, while playing his little fiddle, he raised his sapphire eyes skyward and his hair fell in dark ringlets over his shoulders, he resembled some angel from a heavenly choir.

And so beautifully did Prince Godfrey play his little fiddle, a royal vassal's gift, that it was a marvel, for he had not yet attained his seventh spring.

God had given Godfrey not only sky-blue and radiant eyes, but also a radiant soul. Never once did the prince see tears and suffering with indifference. Small as he was, he knew how to comfort and cheer and aid everyone—not only men, but also animals and plants and all living creatures. In his presence none dared harm the tiniest being, and the shiest birds and animals of the forest seemed to know he was their friend and protector, for they did not fear him at all and never fled before him.

Such were his courage and strength that when once

3

a bull, which had broken loose, charged him with lowered horns, Godfrey, instead of taking flight, seized the animal by the horns and held him fast until the servants came a-running.

Everyone loved the little prince, and indulged and pampered him.

The queen lulled him to sleep with song, and wakened him with kisses.

The king, holding the boy on his knees, told him of his famous ancestry and of knights.

The castle steward whittled swords for him and bows from wood, and setting him on a horse, taught him to ride it.

Handmaids decked him with silk and velvet, curled his hair and rolled it into ringlets.

The old nurse told him fairy tales and fed him with dainties.

And what shall be said of the courtiers but that they vied with one another in waiting upon their little master and amusing him—some because they loved him sincerely, others in order to curry favor with the king and queen.

It happened one day that a mighty enemy with a great army attacked the country.

4

The king thereupon took leave of his wife and son, and with a host of his knights departed to defend the boundaries of his realm. In great anxiety and with tears in her eyes, the queen awaited word from her husband. A day passed and then another, but no messenger came from the field of battle. At length, on the third day, a horn sounded at the walls of the castle. Hastily the guards lowered the drawbridge and a knight, bespattered with blood and dust, rode into the courtyard.

The queen came running out to meet him, followed by the entire court. The knight, alighting from his horse, spoke merrily. "Be of good cheer, gracious mistress," he said. "Our troops have routed the enemy, and the king with his knights are pursuing the fugitives. Make ready to receive him, for he will reach the castle at any moment."

The queen was overjoyed, as were also the courtiers and the whole people, and having donned beautiful attire, they prepared to bid the victor welcome with flowers and song.

They did not wait long. Hoofs clattered, armor clanged and the royal knights arrived. But they blew no horns and sang no songs, as befits conquerors;

they rode in silence and great grief. Nor were they led by their gallant, gracious and noble king—his body was carried on mantles by four bareheaded earls. While returning to the castle after routing his foes, he had been struck by the spear of an enemy soldier, lurking behind the trees.

Oh, royal armorer, how did you forge the golden armor, that a traitorous spear should pierce through it and lodge in the leader's heart?

The queen turned white as a lily, clutched her heart, and fell dead in the arms of her maids-in-waiting.

Oh, royal armorer, how did you forge that golden armor?

The king's brother, Prince Gerald, thereupon summoned the foremost vassals to council and addressed them in these terms:

"We have lost the king, my beloved brother, and the queen as well. Our throne has become vacant. What, then, do you counsel me to do, noble lords?"

Thus he spoke, hoping in his heart that the vassals would invite him to ascend the throne. But the earls and barons kept silent, looking toward Roland, "the Righteous," as he was called, for they esteemed him

6

greatly for his valor and great wisdom and his white hair, and always let him speak first in council.

Up rose Roland the Righteous and retorted to the royal brother:

"Your discourse is not to my liking, Prince Gerald. You state that our throne has become vacant, and ask for counsel regarding what to do with it. Now, has the king not left us Prince Godfrey, his son and rightful successor?"

Thus he spoke and all the knights concurred.

Prince Gerald did not relish this, but hiding his vexation with a smile, he declared:

"You did not understand me, Roland, nor you, noble knights. I well know and do not deny that Godfrey is the rightful successor to the throne. But my nephew is still a little child and it is necessary to appoint a guardian, who shall, until the little prince reaches the age of man, govern the realm and bring up our sovereign to be a worthy knight."

Up rose Baron Ivor, Prince Gerald's trusted friend and captain of his troop.

"Who but you, Prince, should be Godfrey's guardian?" he said. "Are you not his uncle and the man closest to the throne?"

Thus he expressed himself and Roland and the other knights assented, for it was true that none had a greater right to rule than the royal brother.

So it was that Gerald became Prince Godfrey's guardian and regent of the realm, but at heart he coveted the royal crown and pondered how to rid himself of the little prince.

It was Ivor who suggested a way. One day he said to Gerald: "Do as I advise. On the seashore, surrounded by savage cliffs, there stands a tall tower that was once a watchtower. Send Godfrey there with some trusted soldier and command that he be imprisoned. Tell the lords you have sent him to the castle on the seashore because he is sickly and sea air restores strength and health. The frail child will not withstand the prison's discomforts. He will be homesick and lonely, and will surely die. Whereupon, pretending great sorrow, you will bury him with royal honors and obtain the crown for yourself. You alone will then have a right to it."

Thus spoke this wicked villain, and Prince Gerald listened to him gleefully, because the servitor was indeed worthy of his master.

Tale 2

¶ *From the prison where he shall be confined by a kinsman and guardian, he shall be delivered by birds, and shall cross the sea on their wings.*

T was a dismal tower wherein God-frey was imprisoned. All around it rose steep rocky cliffs, and below it roared the green and angry sea, its billows crashing furiously against the rocks and throwing up sprays of white foam.

Not a tree, not a flower, not even a blade of grass was anywhere to be seen. People called these rocks accursed, for not even moss would grow on them. So villagers never passed that way, children never came to play on the shore or search for seashells, fishermen never cast their nets there; even the sea gulls shunned the place.

The bare walls of Godfrey's cell were not adorned with hangings. A little pile of rotted straw had been thrown on the floor for a bed. The tiny window did not let in much light, although it had not been fitted with bars, as none but a bird could escape from such a height.

Many a time Godfrey sat at the window and looked far and wide, hoping to see a passer-by or a fisher-man's boat. But all around there were only emptiness and desolation. There were only the prolonged wailing of the wind and the sound of the waves crashing on the rocky beach.

Twice a year, however, Prince Godfrey had visitors.

In the late autumn birds heading south flew past his tower, and they passed it again in the spring, homeward bound.

"Good day, storks," called the little prince, opening the window. "Whither are you flying?"

"To Egypt, to Egypt, where the blue Nile flows and the tall pyramids rise," answered the storks, but Godfrey did not understand their speech.

"Welcome, swallows, welcome," he called to the passing swallows.

"Hail to you, little boy," answered the swallows, but the little prince did not know they were speaking to him.

"Is it you, larks? Is it you, nightingales? Will you be returning soon?"

"In the spring, in the spring, when the trees are green and the anemones bloom," replied the larks and nightingales.

"How lovely is your song," Godfrey would exclaim, not suspecting that the birds understood him.

14

The cranes always were the last to fly, groaning and whining, and their wings filled Godfrey's heart with sadness, for he knew that thereafter he would remain alone for long, long months.

But one day, and this came to pass in the autumn when the birds were flying out to sea, a wicked boy, aiming his sling, hit one of the swallows. The poor little bird strained to keep up with its companions despite its pain, knowing if it fell along the way it would surely freeze to death in the snow. But just as it came to the tower, the swallow's strength failed completely and the bird dropped on the window ledge with a plaintive peep.

The prince examined its injured wing, carefully removed the sharp pebble, and with a piece of cloth torn from his shirt bathed and bound up the wing. Then he laid the little bird gently on the straw and sat beside it, comforting it with endearing words.

For three weeks Godfrey nursed the swallow, feeding it crumbs of bread, and at the end of the third week the wing had healed. Still, it was not possible to let the bird go, for it was cold outside and he knew the swallow would surely freeze to death. Thus

Prince Godfrey had a companion, and although it was tiny it was so full of twitter, so gay and nimble that it drove all troubles away from the prince.

Before long the little bird had learned to eat out of Godfrey's hand and to fall asleep on his breast. The two played tag and hide-and-seek. The prince could never catch the swallow, who would straightaway fly upward, perch on a stone just under the vault, and thence look down mischievously, squinting one mocking eye. But the bird could catch Godfrey in no time, nipping his hair with its bill. No better did the prince fare at hide-and-seek, for it was easy for the swallow to hide in some dark nook, or some cranny in the wall, while Godfrey could scarcely do the same, as there was nothing in his cell but the bare walls. True, he once tried to conceal himself in the straw on the floor, but there was not enough to cover him entirely and one of his hands showed from under it. The swallow was quick to notice this and, twittering loudly, it began to throw aside straw after straw— so clever was the imp.

At other times Godfrey played his fiddle to the bird. And what do you think? When he played gay tunes, the swallow would spin dancing in the air;

but when in a sad song he complained of his lot, the swallow would come to perch on his shoulder and, tilting its little head right and left, would peer into his eyes and stroke his face with its wing, as if to say: "Do not worry. I am with you and I love you dearly."

Thus the winter passed. The birds began to return from beyond the sea, floating in long ribbons past the prince's tower, amid a whirring of wings and cheerful twitter.

Now the swallow grew sad.

No longer did it play with the prince and rouse him from sleep with its chirping. For days it would touch no food and only sat at the window, motionless, with drooping feathers.

Prince Godfrey grew dejected, too, for he well perceived what the swallow wanted. It was spring and somewhere, far away from the accursed rocks, meadows and fields were green and crocuses bloomed.

Yet should he set the swallow free? He had nothing else in the world.

Should he let it go? If he did, he would be as lonesome and forlorn as he was before.

But could he keep it in confinement? Could he deprive the swallow of fields, meadows and woods, of sunshine, of winged companions, of freedom—of all the things he himself would never see again?

So one day, having kissed the bird, Prince Godfrey opened the window and set it free. Spreading its wings wide, the swallow soared up and away with a gay twitter. The little prince gazed after it until it had vanished from sight.

Once more he was alone. All alone. His only friend had left and forgotten him. And when in the autumn it would again fly past his tower, headed for a warm country, it surely would not even know him. So thought Godfrey, and he was so overcome with grief that he threw himself face down on the floor and burst into loud sobs.

But he was mistaken. The swallow did not forget.

One autumn night the little prince could not fall asleep, because the wind howled and whistled and the sea roared awesomely. When at last he fell asleep, he had a strange dream. He dreamed he was now in his parents' castle, now in prison, he didn't know which—as sometimes happens in a dream. His nurse was at his side telling him a favorite tale, the one about the flying carpet. She had hardly commenced

18

to speak when each of her words changed into a bird and all the birds, with wings extended, laid themselves side by side. Even as Godfrey watched, the birds disappeared and their wings merged into a beautiful, richly patterned, many-colored carpet.

"Lie down on this carpet," said the nurse, "and it will carry you wherever you please."

Godfrey was about to obey her, but at that very moment he awakened. He got up from his miserable straw bed, feeling more wretched than ever. How wonderful it would be, he thought, if he could have such a carpet and could fly forth from this tower to some remote land.

Thus musing, he seated himself at the window in his accustomed manner, and gazed into the distance. Suddenly he observed great flocks of birds heading toward his window in a merry twitter. But this time they did not fly on past him; instead they halted, and with widespread wings settled in the air side by side. Prince Godfrey could not believe his eyes; a many-colored carpet was formed from their wings, iridescent with the red of bullfinches, the blue and green of tits, the black of swallows, the yellow of thrushes, bordered, as if with dainty lace, by the silvery wings of gulls.

Prince Godfrey stared; there was the magic carpet hovering outside his window and beckoning him to flight.

Without another thought Godfrey seized his fiddle, climbed out of the window and jumped, landing on the outspread wings. The magic carpet swayed once and then floated off.

Prince Godfrey looked about. Over his head was boundless sky; below was the immeasurable vastness of the sea. Soon his prison tower was only a speck in the distance.

He knew then that at last he was free, and he stretched out his hands and shouted with all his might. His happiness went to his head like wine, and his heart fairly burst.

When he was somewhat calmer, he leaned back on the wings of the birds, and struck up on his fiddle a song of thanksgiving to God.

Heavenward soared that song, so pure it was, so prayerful, so silvery and glowing that St. Peter, the celestial gatekeeper, although he dislikes the earthly din, and diligently shuts the gates of heaven, opened them wide, that the song might ascend straight to the throne of the Lord.

And St. Michael, the leader of the archangel host, who in golden armor stands guard over the celestial castle, cautiously lifted up his long sword that clanks against the rainbow-colored shining walls, so as not to make the slightest noise.

And the angel choirs left off singing and listened, holding their breath.

And St. Cecilia, too, listened in great admiration and amazement, for even she could not play more beautifully.

And Christ walking thoughtfully amid white lilies in the garden of paradise paused and turned His gentle, pensive eyes toward the earth, seeking the player.

And as His gaze rested upon the carpet of birds which carried Godfrey, the birds marveled that they did not feel the boy's weight, nor any fatigue.

Meanwhile the glow of sunset had come and gone over the sea, the sky had darkened, and the stars began to appear one by one.

Godfrey looked up at the sky that sparkled with a thousand silver lights, and it seemed to him that the eyes of angels gazed down upon him and that one of them, his mother, was laying her lovely, sweet hand over his eyes. And so he fell asleep on the wings of the birds, rocking between sky and sea.

Tale 3

₵ *In a strange, far-off land, clad not in silk or velvet, but in sackcloth, he shall tend sheep.*

HEN Godfrey awoke on the morrow, the golden dawn had already dispelled the darkness. He rubbed his eyes and looked about. There were neither birds nor sea, only huge, snow-capped mountains in the distance, and he was alone again, lying in a green meadow. Godfrey started to his feet, and glanced up, just in time to see the last of the departing birds. They happened to be gulls and the rising sun was tinting their white wings with rose and gold. He perceived then that the birds had laid him down here while he slept, and had then flown onward.

Somehow Godfrey felt lonesome and worried. Whither should he turn? Whither should he wander? How would he make his way by himself in the vast, strange world?

He picked up his fiddle, which the birds had placed on the ground at his side, and smiled sadly. The fiddle, he thought, is my only faithful friend and all I have in the world.

He stroked the fiddle tenderly and the fiddle wept plaintively, moaning and lamenting.

The sorrowful tune floated out, echoed by the

25

mountains from meadow to meadow and from vale to vale.

Little herdboys heard it—those who tended merry goats, grave cows jingling their bells, and shy little white sheep. The shepherds heard it and asked one another: Who might this fiddler be who roams the mountains and plays so as to make the heart in the bosom cry? Let us go and see.

And they followed the sound of the music, driving ahead of them with their long staves the merry goats, the grave cows jingling their bells, and the shy little white sheep.

The old herdsman, too, he who might have been a hundred years old and was the herdboys' guardian and chief when they went with their herds into the mountains for the whole summer, was roused from his musing. And as he listened his heart was so gripped by the tune that although he seldom went out of his hut, he, too, set off to see where the music was coming from.

When they arrived at the dell from which came the sound of the music, they found a tiny lad, lovely as an angel, with starry eyes blue as sapphires, standing alone and playing a fiddle. They formed a circle around him and as they listened they were so over-come with the sadness of the tune he played, that first one, then another, had to wipe away his tears with the sleeve of his shirt.

The cows and sheep stood about sadly and the goats did not even think of their pranks. And every-one was reminded of something sad: one that his little sister had died the spring before; another that there was no bread in his hut; still another that he would have no sheepskin for the winter; another that he had lost the peacock feather from his cap.

Then a cow remembered how they had taken her calf from her, and a sheep recollected how she had gone astray in the mountains and had nearly been snatched by a wolf; a goat recalled how she had sneaked into a cabbage garden and had been trounced out by the shepherd's crook.

The old herdsman, for his part, remembered that he had long since buried his wife, that his sons had wandered forth into the world and he had been left behind, all alone on earth, and there would be no one to close his eyes when the time came for him to die.

But in Godfrey's heart, meanwhile, a kind of cheer-fulness and hope began to rise. What! Was he a sniveler, or some coward that he should so dread the vast world? And, indeed, why was his fiddle weeping so, and lamenting? Should it not rather rejoice because the sky was so clear, the meadows so green, the brooks so silvery, and he himself so free?

And he let his bow dance across the strings.

Ho! It was gay music that now rang out! So lusty and spirited, jolly and merry, that everyone forgot what ailed him.

The shepherds stamped their feet and what a dance they danced. And how the sheep and the goats gamboled, and even the cows—though slowly and with dignity.

The old herdsman held his sides; after all, he was not as old as he seemed. He was still hale, still sturdy, and even now could hop better than many a youngster. Hey, ho!

And the fiddle played on even more giddily, merrily, and lustily.

Presently the birds in the air, and the fish in the water, and the clouds in the sky, were also dancing. And the trees nearly burst with anger because they were rooted in the ground and could not dance.

At last the shepherds cried to Godfrey, "For God's sake, boy, stop, for if you go on playing in this manner, the mountains will move off their bases and start to dancing."

Godfrey laughed and flung up his bow. The old herdsman addressed him thus: "Gracious player, for such music you ought to be rewarded with white bread, honey and wine. But, dear me, we have neither white bread, nor honey, nor wine. However, if you do not scorn black bread, milk and cheese, come along with us."

Godfrey went along eagerly, for he was beginning to feel exceedingly hungry and thirsty.

The shepherds seated him under a shady tree, gave him milk in an earthen cup and freshly picked berries on a fern leaf, while the herdsman fetched him bread and cheese.

The shepherds were well pleased with their guest and were curious to know who he was, where he had come from, where he was bound. But the old herdsman did not let them question Godfrey.

"It ill becomes us," he said, "to bother a wayfarer before he has rested himself and stilled his hunger and thirst."

When Godfrey had finished eating, the herdsman inquired, "Whence do you hail, gracious fiddler, and whither are you bound?"

"I come from a distant land beyond the sea," replied the little prince, "and I am headed whither my eyes take me."

"Gentle player," asked the astonished herdsman, "are you not going to join your kinfolk or friends?"

"My parents are dead," answered Godfrey. "Nor have I any kinfolk or friends. I am going whither my eyes take me."

The herdsman thought for a while and spoke thus: "Would you not stay with us, lad? You shall play your fiddle and we will share with you all we have."

And the herdboys joined in begging and coaxing: "We will teach you to carve pipes out of a willow. We will take you into the woods to pick berries and mushrooms. We will make you elm sandals, and give you the prettiest sheep from our flock to graze."

So Godfrey abided with them, and never regretted having done so.

Life in the mountains was gay indeed, notwithstanding frequent cold and hunger. Godfrey speedily learned to climb trees and rocks, to leap over foaming mountain streams, to kindle fire, to retrieve lost sheep by following their trail, to rise at the crack of dawn, and fall asleep on a bed of leaves as the stars rose. The shepherds loved him well for his good heart and his delightful tunes, and each one, whether at play or at meals, was eager to yield his place to Godfrey.

But Godfrey would always step aside, never attempting to curry favor.

The old herdsman also was very fond of him. He had weathered many a storm, so he would smile and shake his head when he heard the boys discuss how, when they had grown up, they would destroy the wolves who carried off their sheep, or how they would become farmers and till their soil. He could not forget an event which occurred a year after Godfrey had come wandering into the mountains, and which filled him with wonder. It happened thus: One day grooms from a near-by castle had driven up a herd of horses for watering. There was among them a beautiful steed the like of which man's eyes had scarcely seen. He had a mane that shimmered like silver and was soft as silk, flaming and proud eyes, delicate and quivering nostrils, slender legs—in short, he was a

31

marvel. Godfrey, when he saw the horse, could not wrest his eyes from the splendid animal, and at once pleaded with the grooms to let him ride the horse.

The grooms laughed and said, "No one can mount this horse. Twelve knights have tried to tame him and each was thankful to escape with sound limbs. This is a devil, not a horse. Our master nearly killed him once in great anger and despair. He took pity on him only because he is so handsome."

So the grooms talked, but Godfrey paid no heed, and merely stared at the horse as he would at a rainbow. His eyes gleamed like a wildcat's, his nostrils widened, and his face paled and grew flushed by turns. Suddenly he darted toward the horse, and before the grooms could utter a cry he had leaped on the creature's back.

The horse immediately broke into such a frantic gallop that Godfrey merely flashed past their eyes, charging about the meadow at lightning speed. The horse thrust his hoofs into the ground and reared. Everybody closed their eyes, for already it seemed to them that Godfrey was lying on the ground with his head smashed; but they were mute with amazement when presently they saw that he still sat astride the frenzied horse, erect, unafraid and without so much as one hair ruffled. The horse himself seemed astonished. For a few minutes he stood still and motionless, then, apparently seized with rage, he flung himself to the right and to the left, he plunged and bucked and reared, he sped like one possessed straight toward the rocks, hurled himself on the ground with a piercing scream quite unlike a neigh, and frothed white foam at the mouth. But in vain. Godfrey was still astride him, calm, cool and straight as an arrow; his hands were not even holding the mane. In the end the horse grew weary and ceased to buck, whereupon Godfrey rode him around the meadow three times. The boy alighted nimbly and, as if nothing had happened, made for the hut to fetch his fiddle, for he had promised the grooms a new tune.

The old herdsman shook his head.

"Ah, he will not tend sheep with us long," he said. "He is destined to be a great knight, such as the world has never seen." Tears came to his eyes, for he did not know himself how he would live without Godfrey and his tunes.

Godfrey's music was achieving ever greater fame.

From farthermost villages farmers came to hear and invited Godfrey to visit them in the winter when the shepherds returned to the valleys. Knights from neighboring castles likewise came to hear him and wanted to take him along to their courts, but Godfrey would not part from the herdboys. So he continued to live with them, passing the summer in the mountains and the winter in the cottages of the farmers.

And the mountain people had grown so fond of his songs that no christening or wedding could do without him.

Tale 4

℄ *Lured by elves, he shall be saved from dire danger by the miraculous power of his songs.*

MONG the flock which Godfrey tended with the herdboys there was a little goat to which he had taken a particular fancy. It was a beautiful animal. It had long, silky, white hair, black eyes, bright and gay. Always capering, always frisking, the goat had more than once entertained the shepherds with droll pranks; but it caused them no end of trouble because of the way it used to straggle from the flock and make them search long for it in the rocks and thickets. One day, however, it disappeared for good, and the boys could discover no trace of it. The shepherds searched for the goat one day, then the next day and a third day, and at length gave up.

"Evidently," they said, "the wolves have devoured it, so there is no use looking further."

But one bright and moonlit night, such as frequently occurs in July, Godfrey, who was sleeping by the fire with the other herdboys, awoke and heard what sounded like the faraway tinkle of a bell. He raised himself on his elbow and listened. There was no mistaking it; the little goat must be close by. That was its bell which had a special ring, quite distinct

37

from the others in the flock, for the herdsman had bought it only a week before in the market place.

Godfrey jumped up and, without waking anyone, ran in the direction from which the sound came.

Though an instant before it had seemed to him that he heard it coming from no more than a dozen steps away, after he had crossed the clearing where his companions slept and penetrated deeper into the shrubbery, he perceived that the bell sounded somewhere off in the woods. He followed the sound, but instead of getting closer, it began to seem fainter and fainter. Apparently the goat had gone deeper into the woods.

"Jolly, Jolly," Godfrey shouted, for the little animal was gentle beyond measure and used to run up to him instantly when he called.

But it was no use. The bell was farther and farther away and soon Godfrey could hardly follow it.

Finally he was so tired that he was obliged to stop and catch his breath. The goat must have stopped too, for just then Godfrey heard the bell again. And now it seemed very close—a few steps away. Nay, not a few steps. No more than one. A leap would surely bring him to its side.

He leaped. There was no trace of the goat, but again the bell sounded in the distance. Godfrey was so angered that he stamped his foot on the ground. Suddenly soft laughter came from the thicket. It was precisely as if someone were mocking him. Godfrey was puzzled: Was it some forest imp that was teasing him?

The large black trees that stood in the pale moonlight, and the stillness and emptiness, made him uneasy. Strange shadows seemed to be creeping among the branches.

Perhaps he should turn back? Perhaps it was not really the goat, but some forest sprite that had lured him onward into the forest?

Yet he plainly heard the goat's bell, and now it seemed to him that he even heard its bleating. It would be a shame to quail and leave the animal to the mercy of the forest wolves. So Godfrey ran along past the thinning trees and soon came to a little glade.

What now? There was no trace of the goat, but the same laughter rang out anew, this time even louder and nearer. Godfrey glanced about, and suddenly found himself surrounded by a band of dwarfs with butterfly wings at their shoulders and peaked red caps on their heads. They began to dance around him, and rejoiced and exulted until they made the forest ring.

Godfrey recalled how the old herdsman had once related that on moonlit nights elves entice shepherd boys by imitating the bells of lost sheep, and then make the boys dance in their company till morn. He told, too, how elves can dance without a breathing spell, and there is no way to show them that one is weary. Because they themselves do not know fatigue, they will not let the others rest, so that more often than not such a hapless shepherd boy is found dead at dawn.

Ah me, Godfrey thought, I must use my wits, or I shall perish.

Making a graceful obeisance to the elves, he said: "Gentle woodsmen, I see that you wish to dance with me, but truly I am a better player than dancer. Would it not be better that I play a tune for you instead of dancing with you?"

And he took up his fiddle, which he always carried with him in a bag.

The elves were overjoyed because they love music

42

above all else. And every one of them understood that it is one thing to listen to a fiddle and quite another to listen to frog music, with which they usually had to be content. Forthwith they consented and Godfrey began to play blithely and cheerfully as he alone could.

Not only elves came to listen to him, but jack-o'-lanterns and nymphs and all the sundry wood folk, too.

Roe-deer and skittish hares peeped through the branches.

A green lizard crawled out of the grass, wiggled its tail, and winking its eyes roguishly, said to a snail, "Wouldn't you care for a hop, good fellow?"

And the snail, though naturally grave and slow, curiously popped its head out of its shell and waggishly bobbed its little horns.

They danced and frolicked and kept asking for new songs. Godfrey played them one and another, and a third and still another, and finally bowing to the whole assembly, he prepared to return to the clearing where he had left his companions. But the elves had not the slightest inclination to let him go, instead they kept calling for new songs.

Oh, that's bad, thought Godfrey. They will make me play myself to death, just as they have danced the others to death. I must use some stratagem or they will not let me out of here till morning, and I can hardly keep my bow moving over the strings as it is.

So he began a lullaby. And this song made all the foresters so sleepy that each one lay down wherever he could and fell asleep. Even the owls and the nighthawks and the moths dozed off, although it is common knowledge that these gentry are not in the habit of sleeping by night. Only the elves would not yet be lulled to slumber, though they were going around more and more slowly to Godfrey's tune.

When, however, Godfrey began to play a song that described the scented pillows in the cups of flowers, where it was so good and pleasant to stretch out on the soft downy beds while the breeze caressingly rocked them to sleep, the elves, too, were overcome by sleep.

Thus Godfrey was able to rejoin the herdboys, well pleased that he had happily surmounted this predicament.

Greatly did his companions marvel at his adventure when he told it to them in the morning.

Even more amazed was the old herdsman.

And I, Johannes Sarabandus, marveled most of all when the old herdsman recounted it to me years later. Indeed, I know from books of magic that the elves are a malicious and spiteful people and not easy to approach, and I should marvel even more and longer at the power which resided in the songs of this lad had not the old herdsman told me a far more wondrous story about him, the boy, which you shall presently hear.

Tale 5

℄ He shall free mountain
dwellers and little shepherds
from a savage werewolf and
from witches.

SHORT time after the disappearance of the shepherds' pet had involved Godfrey in his adventure with the elves, two other goats went astray, then a ram and four sheep, and last a large white cow, the pride of the whole herd.

The old herdsman brooded greatly over this loss and was particularly disconsolate over the cow. He was angry at the herdboys because they had a mind for nothing but pranks, he said, and could not keep their animals from harm.

When, however, shortly after that, a bull was lost, too, a bull so strong and stubborn that he would have been a match for any wolf, the old man shook his head sadly and said, "Ah, boys, 'tis some unholy power and not the wolves. As long as only goats and sheep were lost, I thought it was your carelessness that was to blame, for it is well known that they are foolish, flighty and thoughtless creatures and likely to come to grief, so that they want careful watching. But with a cow it is an altogether different matter. And what a cow, mind you. Quiet, sedate, not at all given to pranks and frolic. Still, I said to myself that

49

even such a cow might be frightened into straying from the herd, and in the woods a mishap is easily met with. But a bull. Why, he would throw a wolf, and not the other way around."

He had scarce finished speaking when shepherds from the valley next to theirs came running and began to inquire if their neighbors had seen two cows from their own herd—one black, they said, and the other piebald.

They proceeded to complain and lament that things had been getting out of hand lately, so many cattle had disappeared under their very eyes. And not only that. Why, only yesterday two shepherds had gone into the woods to search for sheep, and had not yet returned.

Likewise, they said, farmers from near-by villages have come to us to inquire about children. It appears that they went picking berries and were lost. But, stranger yet, yesterday at evenfall there came hurrying into our valley the wife of John the Sharpshooter, who is known as the best shot of the neighborhood, and she told us, crying, that three days have gone by since he went chamois-chasing and he has not yet come home. No doubt about it, some mighty packs of hungry and very daring wolves must have come sneaking from the other side of the mountains.

The old herdsman listened to this tale in gloomy silence, and then said, "Nay, not wolves; they are not wolves that go ravening hereabouts; it is a werewolf and his devilish crew that are stalking about. We shall all perish pitifully, we and our herds."

A great terror came over the shepherds. They all grew silent, casting fearful glances at one another. Godfrey, however, was not a whit alarmed. He began to inquire curiously about the werewolf and his crew who frightened everybody. But the old herdsman responded thus:

"It does no good talking about it. Empty talk will avail nothing and calamity is easily invited. Be on your guard. Stay close to one another. Do not scatter and God grant that we somehow come through scatheless, for an evil creature does not like a crowd." The herdboys obeyed him and none dared leave his companions to go picking raspberries or mushrooms, while at night they huddled together like frightened sheep.

Laughter and gay talk ceased. Melancholy and fear came to reign among them. Godfrey alone did not lose his spirit, and his gay songs bore up his companions' hearts.

A few days passed in complete quiet and soon the shepherds began to take heart. Perhaps the evil was past.

First one, then another, made bold enough to stray from his companions in order to drive in a goat or to seek out some special tree for reeds.

But the wicked being did not sleep; it merely lay in wait, the better to deceive the watchful shepherds. And so it was that Jackie the Homeless, so nicknamed because he was an orphan and had no one in the world, disappeared one day without leaving a trace. He was Godfrey's dearest comrade. Dismay struck everybody, and Godfrey, despite the shepherd's interdiction, sought long and singly for his cherished companion, weeping and greatly sorrowing for him. Finally, when he returned to camp without finding the boy, he vowed in his heart he would destroy the monster. He said nothing about his decision to anyone, but constantly kept thinking of how he was going to find the werewolf.

By chance he soon found an opportunity.

52

One day there arrived in the valley a farmer from a far-off village in the mountains. Bowing to the herdsman, he said that he had heard of the great player from his shepherds and had come expressly to bid him to a wedding. This request did not surprise the herdsman and his boys, for, as I have said already, the fame of Godfrey's songs had spread far and wide over the region and no wedding or christening could be held without his music.

The old herdsman prided himself upon having such a player among his herders, and would gladly have given his permission. But something about this farmer did not please him; the man was shaggy like a wolf and all clothed in skins, he flashed his eyes like a wild beast, and his smile was sly and malevolent.

The old man was loath to let Godfrey go along with the stranger, therefore he took the boy aside and said, "I do not know what manner of man this is, but he has something evil in his eyes, and times are uncertain. Also, I heard my grandfather say that a werewolf can sometimes assume man's shape, the more easily to deceive and trick people. I do not like to see you go off into the mountains and wild woods

53

with this stranger, but it would be most painful for me to deny his request. After all, he may be a very good fellow, and, as he said himself, he has come a great distance."

Godfrey was well pleased to hear these words, and thought, Grant God it is the werewolf and not a peasant from the far away mountains. I do not know yet what I am going to do, but one thing I do know: his fiendish mischief will not go unpunished.

To the herdsman he said aloud, "An old mountaineer who used to come to the valley for milk and cheese told me, .too, how werewolves sometimes prowl about in human shape. But he also said they feel ill at ease in the skin of man and can easily be discovered then. For, to make themselves more comfortable, they often cast it off like an ill-suited garment, and in so doing flash a bloodshot eye or a wolf's claw. This man, however, does not act in that manner. Besides, why should he assume man's shape to lure away a little shepherd like me? Could he not, if he wished, just carry me off and do away with me, as he has done with Jackie the Homeless? He is only a common peasant, and he is hairy and ill-clad as peasants from wild mountainous regions sometimes are. It would not be right, I think, to hurt him with such suspicions and refuse his request."

"Go along with him, then, if that is your will," said the herdsman. "I will not cross you, although some uneasiness is troubling me."

Godfrey thereupon took his fiddle and, bidding farewell to the old herdsman and the boys, set forth with the stranger.

They had not gone a long way when the stranger said to Godfrey, "The sun is scorching hot today. I must take off my cap and my sheepskin."

He removed his cap and there appeared from under it not hair, but something like a wolf's pelt.

He doffed his sheepskin and his shirt which was open on his chest revealed a body covered with hair like that of a beast.

He wiped his sweaty forehead with his hand and it was as if suddenly his hand had changed to a beast's paw.

Ho, ho! thought Godfrey, but he did not say a word.

They walked on and after a while Godfrey's companion began to complain that his shoes were greatly troubling him.

55

"Take them off, sir," said Godfrey, "and you will feel more comfortable."

To which the other answered, "I would take them off gladly, only I am afraid you might be frightened when you see my feet."

"Why should I be frightened?" asked Godfrey, feigning great surprise.

"Well—because my feet are not like those you are used to."

"Why?" said Godfrey, shrugging his shoulders. "Have you hoofs on your feet, or what?"

"Well, not quite hoofs. But constant walking in the mountains has given me corns and bumps which make them look like hoofs."

"I know well how the skin sometimes toughens from walking barefoot and I am not frightened by any such thing. My grandfather had such corns on his feet that they looked like two gnarled stumps. Why shouldn't yours look like hoofs? So take them off without another thought."

The stranger was greatly pleased. "You are a clever lad," he said. And sitting down on a stone he removed his shoes. Instead of toes on his feet there were hoofs just like those of devils, only so large that Godfrey was quite astonished. Yet he showed no sign of it, but smiled and said, "Hah, you are a sissy, sir. My grandfather had larger bumps and he did not groan as you do."

Thus he spoke while within him great anger welled up, and rage choked him, for he now knew for certain what kind of farmer ·this was. And he would have leaped at the werewolf's throat then and there, but he remembered Jackie the Homeless, and thought: No, dear comrade, you shall not be unavenged. This cruel monster shall inflict no more harm on mankind. I will not be done away with for nothing. I will wait for a favorable moment and hold my anger in leash until I accomplish my design.

So they marched on all day and all night and at last they reached the devil's abode where the werewolf and his cronies, the witches and ogres, dwelt. It stood in the midst of steep and bare rocks, in a small and weirdly dismal glen. Godfrey was quite weary by the time they reached it, for the journey had been arduous, and the werewolf, once he had rid himself of his shoes which cumbered him greatly since he was unaccustomed to human footgear, had run so swiftly that Godfrey could hardly keep pace with him.

Therefore, when they came to the valley, Godfrey sat down on a stone and said, "You must let me rest awhile, sir."

"Rest yourself," replied the werewolf cheerfully. "Though it surprises me that it is only now you are feeling weary, because from here we can see the roofs of the houses, and the saying is that a horse runs faster once he sees the stable."

So they sat down together, and Godfrey peered about curiously, fixing in his mind every detail of this place.

But, to tell the truth, there was not much to see. It was a barren glen where nothing grew, and its black and hard soil suggested a big threshing floor. There was a small but deep lake almost at the far end of it, and beyond the lake there rose a hillock, huddled up against the rocks that enclosed the glen. On this very hillock the werewolf and his henchmen had put up their huts.

"What lake is that?" inquired Godfrey of the werewolf.

"That lake is called the Loch of the Drowned," returned the werewolf.

And Godfrey at once recalled what the old herdsman had told him about the lake: "The water is deep even at the shore and its mysterious whirlpools draw in the best swimmers. Nobody has ever yet come out of the lake alive."

"Well, let us go," said the werewolf, rising. "It is a pity to waste time. Indoors you will rest and refresh yourself."

They skirted the lake and started to climb up the hill where the devils' huts stood. These did not differ much from the usual peasant huts, except that they had no windows and their walls were not whitened with lime, but were blackened with tar, since evil spirits do not like white.

Each of the huts was surrounded, as is common in the country, by a little garden. But they were queer gardens, indeed. Instead of sunflowers, cats' heads grew on tall stalks and peeped intently at passers-by, blinking their gleaming, green eyes. The trees had leaves shaped like outstretched human fingers which kept curling up and straightening out, and row on row, like neatly planted cabbage-heads, grew bearded muzzles of black bucks. About the porches coiled something that looked a bit like peas and a bit like wild vine. When, however, Godfrey looked at this plant more closely he noted that its climbing stalks moved continually like a tangle of green snakes, and its flowers, shaped like long red tongues, hid and showed again, smacking greedily.

Another lad would surely have fainted with terror at such a sight, but Godfrey knew no fear. He was merely seized with loathing and great disgust but he never so much as trembled, being well aware that the werewolf was watching him intently. At last the monster stopped in front of one of the cottages and, opening the gate, entered the garden. Here he was greeted by an old dame, lean as a rod, with a thick mop of bristling hair on her head. Godfrey gazed at her, wondering what sort of freak this was, then realized that she was nothing but a plain broom prettily dressed in a skirt and bodice.

"This is the handmaid of my betrothed," said the werewolf. "She is an industrious and good girl."

And the broom began to wriggle coyly and preen herself and giggle, and veil herself with her apron, as village maidens will do.

"I am going," she said, "to give the bats a drink, because evening is falling and our cattle will wake anon."

Meanwhile the werewolf entered the cottage, so Godfrey followed him.

The room was completely dark, except for a fire that burned in the middle of it. In its red light Godfrey beheld a witch seated by the fire. Her face was as yellow as a lemon, her eyes gleamed like those of a cat and she had a long hooked nose and one green tooth which stuck out of her hideous mouth and reached down to her chin.

The werewolf at once presented Godfrey to her, saying he was the player who had been brought along for the next day's wedding.

"You must be very wayworn and hungry after so long a journey?" screeched the witch in a voice that resembled the squeak of ungreased wheels, "so be seated and eat, for the evening meal is ready."

And she brought forth some pots and cups which were like skulls of men and beasts and were filled with smoking food.

But Godfrey had no stomach for such devils' fare, wherefore he excused himself, saying that fatigue had got the better of his hunger. He lay down in one corner of the room and pretended to fall asleep. Yet, in real truth, he did not sleep at all, but listened closely to the conversation between the witch and the werewolf.

"Why do you take such pains with this one shepherd?" said the witch to the werewolf. "Could you not just snatch him, bring him hither and force him to play, instead of going to all the trouble of putting on the guise of man?"

"Very troublesome it was indeed," answered the werewolf and, shedding the rest of his human guise, he suddenly turned into a huge wolf with shining bloodshot eyes and horse hoofs. "Phew! I can hardly breathe. Still, I could not do otherwise, for had I snatched the boy and dragged him hither, forcing him to play, he would scarcely be alive from fright and his music would not be very gay to dance to. Now, this is to be a wedding the like of which has not yet been witnessed. It isn't every day that a werewolf weds a witch."

Ho, ho, I will treat you to some wedding, thought Godfrey, still pretending to be asleep, and even snoring occasionally.

"You are right," agreed the witch. "You have contrived this wisely. But tell me, what do you propose to do with him afterward?"

62

The werewolf broke into laughter, exhibiting his sharp white fangs and retorted with a grin, "Methinks a roast of the fiddler would be no worse than any other. We will eat him together with that other herdboy whom I carried away from their valley last week."

"I have been trying to fatten him up but he is still as skinny as a lath," said the witch wryly.

At these words Godfrey was overjoyed, and thought: So you are still alive, Jackie dear. Well, please God, I will set you free, and together we shall return safe and sound to the valley.

For he had already formed his scheme to destroy the ogres, witches and the werewolf and deliver the whole region of the devil-sent plague. So he kept listening to what the witch was whispering to the werewolf.

"We are talking too loud," she said. "The boy might hear us."

"Don't be silly," replied the werewolf. "See, he is fast asleep."

And he laughed again.

"He is not so clever. He has not the slightest notion of where he is. He is a frightfully stupid boy."

Godfrey listened no longer. Now that he knew all he wanted to learn, he resolved to rest awhile. He fell asleep and slept soundly not only through that night, but through nearly all the next day as well, so weary was he from the exertion of the journey.

He was at length aroused by the preparations which the witch and the werewolf, aided by the broom, were making for the wedding.

"We shall have to clear the room," said the witch, "because once the dancing gets under way we will need every bit of space."

"That will not help much," sighed the werewolf. "The room is so small and the guests will be many."

"I know a way to avoid a crush," remarked Godfrey unexpectedly, for he had been listening closely to the conversation.

"Now, what would you suggest?" queried the werewolf.

"If you want my advice," said Godfrey, "then do not dance indoors, but down in the valley by the lake. It is going to be a moonlit night, there will be plenty of room for dancing, and since there are no bushes or stones and the ground is level and hard, you will be more comfortable than inside. You can dance in the

valley on one side of the lake while I stand on the other, on the hill, and play for you. Because of the mountains all around, the music will be echoed loud and clear throughout the valley."

"By my dear devil!" exclaimed the werewolf, who had forgotten that he was supposed to be a peasant. "By my dear devil, the lad is right."

The witch, however, was possessed of more sagacity than the werewolf, a woman being commonly shrewder than a man. So she said to Godfrey, "That is good advice about the valley. But tell me, why is it you want to stand on the other side of the lake when you play right amongst us in the valley?"

"I will explain," replied Godfrey. "You must have heard how, when I strike up a lively tune in my sweeping manner, nobody and nothing can stand still, but all must instantly start to dance and keep at it for as long as their breath holds. Well, if I should be standing in your midst, you would jostle me ever and again and hinder me from playing. And then, too, I would fain watch your dancing, and it will be much easier for me to see you from the hill than if I should stand in the middle of the crush, in the throng."

65

"Have it your way, then," acquiesced the witch, having dismissed her suspicions.

And straightaway she ran off to invite the guests to the valley.

Ugh, 'twas a sight and something to wonder at when the guests began to assemble!

Horrible witches there were galore, those who will harm men in no time, and ogres and bogies which feed on human blood, and goblins who lead travelers astray on foggy nights. In the bright moonlight Godfrey could see clearly from his hill as the gathering paired off for dancing. They were overjoyed at having such a fiddler to play for them, for usually at devils' weddings the only music is the whistling of the wind and the croaking of toads.

Well, thought Godfrey, with God's help this shall be your last dance. And he drew the bow across the strings.

Ho! So sprightly and rousing was the music which resounded through the valley that not only the ogres, witches and goblins, led by the werewolf, began to dance; but even the brooms, who, as is well known, are in attendance upon witches, ran out of the huts and started whirling with their mistresses.

66

And the dancing grew ever more frenzied, ever giddier, until the dancers' breath failed, sparks began to fly before their eyes, and reason left their heads.

The witches thrust their claws into one another, and danced on.

The ogres and goblins took each other by the hand and spun about, howling and whistling with glee so loud that the wind scurried all over the valley and the bats, startled by this wild uproar, fled in swarms from the devils' huts.

The brooms lost their skirts and bodices and thrashed about right and left with such fury that from sheer impetus one and then another slashed her mistress on the pate.

In the middle was the werewolf himself, dancing, stamping his hoofs, flashing his bloodshot eyes and showing his sharp fangs.

Ha, you will not rejoice long, son of the devil, thought Godfrey, and struck the strings even more violently.

And the whole fiendish lot surged forward in one solid mass, lured onward by the irresistible call of the dance music and unmindful of the bottomless lake that separated them from the fiddler.

Perhaps one or another would have come to his senses and stopped, but the dance-drunk crowd swept him forward and carried him along.

And the fiddle kept calling from the other shore of the lake, ever louder, ever more insistently.

Onward, onward, this way, this way, the music seemed to say.

Just at the water's edge, the crowd seemed to waver, but drunk with the music and completely senseless, it plunged straight into the lake.

Thus it was that Godfrey freed the whole region of the werewolf, the ogres, witches and goblins—the whole devilish crew. In one of the huts he found Jackie the Homeless and other shepherds whom the werewolf had kept imprisoned, all of whom his music had saved from horrible death.

Great joy reigned in all the valleys and throughout the region, and the fame of Godfrey's songs, which had such power that even the devils could not resist them, spread not only over the mountains but through the length and breadth of the land until it reached the royal court.

Tale 6

⸿ *He shall heal the daughter of a mighty king, and
shall be made a page at the
king's court.*

A T the sound of trumpets and horns everybody ran out—old men and young, women and children. They stood gazing in amazement. There approaching the village was the gracious king himself in the midst of a cavalcade of a hundred horses. Ahead rode the heralds in their silver livery, followed by trumpeters from whose golden bugles floated pink ribbons. Behind the trumpeters came the knights in their resplendent armor, preceding a sleigh drawn by twelve teams of snow-white steeds, and in the sleigh was seated the august king himself.

The heralds halted, ordered the trumpets blown toward the four corners of the earth, and proclaimed the royal command:

"Let the village player, named Godfrey, come forward and stand before the king."

Out of the crowd stepped Godfrey and stood before the king, confused and abashed.

The king was amazed.

"So you are that player whose fame has reached my court?" he exclaimed. "I had expected to see a white-haired old man, and I find instead a little lad, not much older than my Roxana. Play a tune for me and I will reward you generously with gold and silver and with my royal favor."

Godfrey smiled and answered, "I do not trade my songs for gold or silver, but if you have come to hear them, sire, then listen."

And he began to play so enchantingly that the heralds and the knights and the king himself listened with delight.

When Godfrey had finished, King Sigmund exclaimed, "Gentle player, there is, indeed, no greater fiddler than you on earth. You shall not dwell in a mean cottage or in a shepherd's hut. I will take you along to my court, to my castle."

But Godfrey replied, "Truly, gracious King, I am grateful, but I will not go with you."

"Surely you have heard how beautiful my castle is," said the king. "Its vault rests upon a thousand tall columns; its walls are hung with precious draperies, daintily embroidered with flowers of a hundred different hues and streaked with silver; and its floors are covered with soft carpets. A hundred lamps, suspended on golden chains, dispel the darkness of the night. Perfumes, brought from far-off lands, enclosed

72

in silver amphors, send forth exquisite scents. Under my castle are a thousand dungeons and around it rise tall and mighty walls, barring the way to foes."

Pointing to the blue sky, Godfrey said with a ripple of laughter, "Look up, King Sigmund. There is the vault of my castle, and when night falls, not a hundred, but a hundred thousand lamps will flash thereunder. Mark those huge spruces, thick-set and sturdy at the bottom, delicate and slender at the top—those are the columns of my castle. Behold this soft white carpet that covers my floor—did the merchants bring you from the Orient any that surpasses it in beauty? In the spring I shall change it for another of emerald green, embroidered with ever-varying flowers, sparkling with diamonds of dew, a carpet that is fragrant and living. Look at these silent pine trees—they are my amphors whence the perfume of sap is wafted. As for walls, I need none, for I have no foes, King Sigmund. Truly, I will not go with you."

"Unreasonable child, you do not know your good fortune," said the king. "Royal favor is not bestowed every day, mind you. In my castle you will eat from gold and silver plates and my servants will bow low before you."

"Gracious King," Godfrey replied, "the wood serves me ruby-colored berries on dainty fern leaves, and only a fool will barter friends' hearts for the bows of servants."

The august king knitted his brow.

"A thousand vassals, you village player, do my bidding and none of them would dare spurn my invitation. They are all earls and barons of noble blood and great ancestry, and each of them lords it over ten castles."

"A thousand vassals, gracious lord, do your bidding," Godfrey replied, "and they are all earls and barons of noble blood and great ancestry, each lording it over ten castles. What, then, is a simple village fiddler to you?"

The king was seized with great anger.

"Wretched herdboy, your words are very daring," he exclaimed. "Since you do not know the worth of my favor, you shall know my anger. I will order my grooms to drive you to the castle in fetters."

Godfrey turned pale as a lily, but it was not the pallor of fear. He advanced a few steps toward the king and proudly flung back his head, his eyes as cool as a mountain lake.

"You can drive me to your castle in fetters, King Sigmund—it is within your power to do so—but even though you thrust your sword into my breast till it reaches my heart, I swear by my fiddle, not one of my songs shall you hear."

Utter silence fell and none of the courtiers dared to breathe, but trembled, like leaves in a wind.

King Sigmund and Godfrey stared into each other's eyes as if locked in single combat.

And an amazing thing came to pass. Suddenly King Sigmund, the powerful and proud, bent his head and pleaded in a gentle tone, "Forgive my words, Godfrey. They were the words of a distraught father who does not know how to save his child. My only daughter, Princess Roxana, has been stricken with a strange and frightful illness which is called melancholy. The healers tell me that she is being slowly poisoned by sadness and will die ere the buds blossom on the trees. Only one thing can help her—the deep and spontaneous laughter that comes straight from the heart. I thought perhaps you might save her."

"Why did you not tell me so at once, King Sigmund?" exclaimed Godfrey. "Let us lose no time in idle talk, but let us hurry to rescue the princess."

Overjoyed, the king seated Godfrey at his side in the sleigh, wrapped the boy in his own mantle, for the wind was whistling through his shabby sheepskin, and bade the horses started.

While they drove, Godfrey demanded of the king: "Tell me, gracious King, how Princess Roxana came to be stricken with this strange and poisonous melancholy?"

King Sigmund sighed.

"Would that I knew, my boy. Has not my daughter magnificent apartments? Do not a hundred handmaidens await her pleasure? Has she not robes of velvet and silk, of gold and silver brocade? Have I not bestowed upon her the most precious jewels? True, her mother died when Roxana was still in her cradle. But does she want for care? Has she not twelve ladies-in-waiting, who watch her every step? No, indeed, I know not why my daughter is ailing with this strange and poisonous melancholy."

They drove on in silence, then the king asked, "Gentle player, do you chance to know why there is such strange animation in all the villages as if the people were preparing for festivities?"

"Gracious King," replied Godfrey, astonished, "have

78

you forgotten that this evening, at the gleam of the first star, people will sit down to their Christmas supper?"

"My castle is sad and dark," the king said gloomily. "It is a long time since we have celebrated a festivity there. Instead, death stands guard at its gates. Grant God, my lad, that we may break the bread cheerfully today."

And Godfrey said to him with a very grave air:

"Everything is within the power of the Lord, sire, may His name be hallowed on earth and in heaven."

When the king and Godfrey entered the chamber of Princess Roxana, dusk had already fallen and the handmaidens had lighted the candles in the heavy silver candlesticks. This they had done quietly and noiselessly, for every sound jarred the ailing princess.

The walls of the chamber were draped in dark violet, almost black, velvet, embroidered with golden lilies, and the windows were covered with heavy hangings.

The princess lay in a large, richly carved bed, under a damask canopy. Her little face, set in a halo of golden hair, was whiter than the laces of the bedclothes, and her tiny hands, all their strength gone, rested on a rich blanket.

About her, rigid and motionless, as becomes ladies-in-attendance on royalty, sat twelve ladies-in-waiting, who, at the sight of the king, rose simultaneously, curtsied low and then resumed their seats, as rigid and motionless as before.

But the little princess did not even stir. Only her long eyelashes, which cast black shadows upon the transparent whiteness of her cheeks, fluttered a little.

Godfrey looked into her violet, strangely wistful and pensive eyes. "What songs do you like, little Princess?" he inquired.

"I like quiet, sad songs, gray and weeping as an autumn day," she said. "I like such songs and no others, because that is how all about me seems to be, and not otherwise."

The king sighed deeply, but Godfrey wasn't a bit perturbed. He said:

"Very well, Princess, I shall play such a tune for you. Listen."

And he played. A strange song it was indeed.

Bim . . . bum, bim . . . bum, went the patter of the large, heavy raindrops against the windowpanes.

Aaah . . . aaah, plaintively moaned the flowers and blades of grass, bending under their weight.

The wicked gale is tearing us apart. Will the sun never shine? whispered the trees.

Never . . . never . . . never, howled the wind.

Bim . . . bum, bim . . . bum, went the heavy raindrops splashing on the panes.

"I like your tune," said the little princess. "Play on, play on, Godfrey."

And Godfrey played on.

A soft, thin thread of cheer slipped into the somberness of the autumn song.

"What is it, Godfrey?" asked the princess. "What is it, Godfrey?"

"It was a tiny ray of sunshine that peeped from behind the clouds, but it took fright at the darkness and hid again."

"Can it be, can it be, Godfrey? What a coward that little ray is. Poor trees and flowers."

"Ah . . . wait, Princess. It ran back to its brothers and all together they are beginning to drive the clouds away. The gale is ceasing to wail, the flowers are straightening, the trees are merrily shaking the water from their branches, the gray, shaggy clouds are fleeing in terror, a rainbow of seven colors is shining in the sky."

"Oh, brave, beloved sunshine."

"See," said Godfrey, "the sky is blue, a fresh, clear blue. Diamond drops are shining on the dazzling scarlet of the cherries in the orchard, the brook is hopping from stone to stone in a silvery ripple, and the trees and the flowers and the butterfly-winged little elves and the green-haired dryads and even Princess Roxana are beginning to dance, and to laugh, too. Listen: Princess Roxana laughs loudest and gayest of all."

And then they all fell to dancing: the butterflies and the birds, the elves and the flowers, the dryads and the trees. Leaping out of bed, the little princess danced more enchantingly and at a speedier and giddier pace than all the butterflies and the birds and the elves and the flowers and the dryads. Her golden curls flew about her little flushed face, and her tiny feet flickered from under her long white nightgown, chasing each other like two small pink pigeons.

The old king looked on, crying and laughing, and suddenly he, too, jumped to his feet, folded his ermine mantle, and happily joined in the dance. And

82

following the king, went Godfrey with his fiddle.

Only the twelve ladies-in-waiting sat rigid and motionless as becomes ladies-in-attendance on royalty. At length Godfrey stopped, for he was afraid too much activity might harm the princess. He began to play a song about how the sun sets, how the birds return to their nests, how the cups of flowers curl up. And the princess returned to bed.

Godfrey sat by her side and played songs describing how the stars rise and the birds and flowers fall asleep, the trees and the dark mountain lakes and the whole mysterious, wide and unknown world.

The princess fell asleep, and at her side the old king, too, fell asleep in a deep armchair. In the end so did the player himself.

On the morrow when Princess Roxana awoke she was well again, and her first words were, "Will you stay with me forever, Godfrey?"

And looking into her large violet eyes, so sad the day before and so radiant now, Godfrey returned, "I will stay with you forever, Princess."

And he remained at the castle. He was the princess' page and player, and the two children loved each other greatly.

Tale 7

(*Having defeated the conqueror of a hundred tourneys, he shall win his knight's spurs.*

EAR this account of a wondrous and miraculous event, and may the truth of my words be borne out by all those noble dukes, earls and barons who attended the feast tendered by King Sigmund to celebrate his victory over the heathen ruler Suleiman.

Many of those men live no longer, many of them have scattered all over the world, but Arnold of Treville, who met with this adventure, is still alive, so you may ask him, and he will not have the audacity to deny it. I do not, however, advise you to do so for he is a fellow of coarse and ribald manner, having none of the genteel courtliness that suits a knight.

At that feast Princess Roxana, who heretofore, being still a child, had taken no part in the festivities of knights, made her first appearance. Behind her chair, in attendance as her page, stood Prince Godfrey, whose fourteenth spring was then beginning, and across the table facing the princess sat Earl Arnold of Treville who was held in great esteem for his strength and courage and who was very boastful of being the conqueror in a hundred tournaments.

Now, you should know that the royal pages wore

a livery of blue velvet, and each had his coat of arms embroidered in gold on his chest, for they were all lads of noble blood. Only Godfrey had no escutcheon, because no one knew who he was and whence he came.

It so happened that the aforenamed Earl Arnold, having drunk himself tipsy with claret, began to mock Godfrey in an unbecoming manner, for the earl was, as I already stated, a fellow of coarse and ribald habit.

Well then, Earl Arnold said to Godfrey, "I say, royal page, what has become of your coat of arms? Did you lose it somewhere along the way? For I have heard that you have a very beautiful coat of arms—a sheep in a green field and above it two crossed staves."

Godfrey eyed Arnold with a proud look but made no reply.

And Arnold, holding his sides, guffawed and said, "You regard me rather haughtily, my lad. Am I in error? The king brought you as a Christmas gift to the princess, so perchance you have a Christmas star on your escutcheon? Ah, that must be a splendid coat of arms, and a rare one, to boot. No wonder, therefore, that you are so proud."

Godfrey bit his lips until blood showed and turned pale with fury, but returned no answer.

"He, he," Arnold persisted. "Will you permit me to ask you, Knight of the Star of the Nativity, in what region your ancestral castle is situated, because slanderers say that it does not exist at all and that your forefathers looked after swine?"

Princess Roxana knitted her brows, pouting her mouth proudly, and said, "Earl Arnold, even if Godfrey's forefathers did tend swine, they surely must have excelled you in the gentility of their manners."

The king and all the knights laughed loud, and Earl Arnold turned purple with wrath.

"Truly, gentle Princess, there is no need for you to champion your servant so ardently, for he can answer me for himself. Well, now, Godfrey, have you turned deaf, or do you not deign to speak to me?"

But Godfrey kept silent, regarding him with the same contempt. Arnold smote his fist on the table, making the tumblers clink and the boards creak, and exclaimed:

"I see you are asleep on duty, royal page, but I will wake you." And seizing a bone from a dish, he flung it at Godfrey.

The boy stepped forth into the middle of the hall, and drawing a little sword, such as was worn by pages as an ornament, said, "Let the most gracious king and the gentle princess and all the knights here assembled bear witness, I challenge you, Earl Arnold of Treville."

The knights burst into laughter, for it was indeed an amusing spectacle to see that child facing the huge, broad-shouldered man and brandishing his little toy of a sword. And Earl Arnold of Treville laughed loudest of all.

But Godfrey, turning to face the king, began to speak in a voice as strong and ringing as bronze.

"Most gracious King, let justice prevail. Do not suffer the Earl of Treville to walk away with impunity after insulting me. Let him answer for his words according to the rules of knights."

And so grave and dignified was Godfrey's bearing that complete silence came over the gathering and the laughter died on everybody's lips.

The king lifted his head and said with severity: "Earl Arnold of Treville, did you not hear the challenge? I command you to come forward and fight."

As the knights glanced at one another, Arnold stood up and spoke.

"You must be jesting, most gracious lord. You would disgrace me and my clan forever by commanding me to engage this boy. Why, everybody would point his fingers at me, mocking, 'There goes the gallant knight who knocked a sword out of a child's hands.' And if in knocking out his sword, I were to injure him, which might happen to the most skillful swordsman, I should be crushed with shame."

The king, however, replied, "Arnold of Treville, a knight does not insult one weaker than himself. By insulting him you have acknowledged him as your peer. Go, then, and fight."

"Will nothing, most gracious King, alter your determination?" Arnold demanded.

"Nothing, Arnold of Treville."

"And if Godfrey should withdraw his challenge?"

"Only then would I revoke my command."

"Look here, boy," said Arnold threateningly, "you surely understand that I shall knock out your sword at the first stroke. And I warn you—I shall then show you at my sword's point what it means to pit yourself against a knight. Desist from your challenge, and I will give you as much gold as you can carry."

"Earl Arnold," said Godfrey, his eyes aflame, "Earl Arnold, to your previous insults you have added a new one. You shall know, however, that the fate of arms is not in your own but in God's hands. By St. George, step forward, or I will force you into combat at my sword's point, you abject coward."

"Ha, insolent pup," roared Arnold, "defend yourself then."

And he lunged at Godfrey with a cross thrust.

Godfrey shielded himself with his toy sword and miraculously parried the thrust.

A murmur of amazement broke forth from the whole assembly. How was it that the conqueror of a hundred tourneys could not knock out this child's sword at the first stroke? Up rose the knights and formed a circle around the two contestants.

Arnold, almost out of his senses with rage, lunged once more. And once more Godfrey parried his stroke.

Thereupon Arnold lost his self-possession. He felt that all his glory as a knight was crumbling to dust and he knew if he did not win this laughable, childish contest at once, there would be no knight willing to cross swords with him. No longer was he mindful that his opponent was but a child. He kept lunging with grim, vengeful fury. He used his most famous, most difficult-to-parry strokes. But in vain. Godfrey beat back his sword skillfully and with ease, as if this were child's play to him. They grappled for a long time and Arnold's strokes began to weaken and to falter.

And then a shout of astonishment broke forth from all throats: Godfrey had shifted from defense to attack.

For a few moments Arnold, with obvious difficulty, succeeded in warding off his adversary's strokes, but presently he began to retreat.

At that very instant Godfrey abruptly swung his sword in a whirling, masterly flourish, and another cry was uttered by the knights. Arnold's sword spun in mid-air and fell at Godfrey's feet. Godfrey stepped on it.

"The combat is ended, Earl Arnold," he said calmly.

Arnold groaned and covered his face with his hands.

"I am dishonored, gracious King. Strip me of my knight's belt and spurs, for I am unworthy of them. Let me have a distaff and a spindle, for they alone suit me now."

"You are wrong, Arnold," said the king gravely. "We are three hundred knights here, but none could have withstood this child. You may fairly say that you have been defeated only once, but it was by a warrior such as our knights have never known. Godfrey, until now you have had no emblem. Henceforth it shall be the Star of the Nativity. Until now you have had no surname. Henceforth you shall be known as Godfrey the Conqueror. You have been a page. Kneel," the king commanded.

Godfrey knelt and the king, having dubbed him thrice, announced, "I proclaim you a knight."

And the assembled earls and barons acclaimed him, "Long live Godfrey the Conqueror, Knight of the Star of the Nativity."

But Godfrey, still kneeling, looked imploringly at Princess Roxana, and she, grasping the meaning of his look, tore a blue ribbon from her gown and handed it to Godfrey with a smile.

Tale 8

¶ *Without drawing his sword, he shall capture a castle which the king himself and his whole army would not have dared to attempt.*

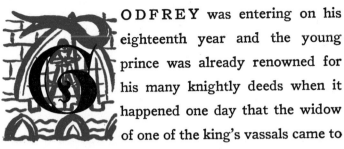

ODFREY was entering on his eighteenth year and the young prince was already renowned for his many knightly deeds when it happened one day that the widow of one of the king's vassals came to King Sigmund's court with a sorrowful complaint. It occurred thus:

After her husband's death, the lord of many neighboring castles had solicited her hand. However, since she bore him no affection, she refused his suit. Whereupon the offended knight seized her domain, burned her castle and drove her out with her little son.

The king was greatly angered by such an act of violence and promised to punish this lawlessness and to restore her manor. But on asking the name of the offender he heard that the man was the Earl of Montclair.

"Gentle lady," he said gloomily, "God bear me witness that I should be most unwilling to see you depart without redress from the throne. Yet what am I to do when it is not in my power to fight Earl Albert? He lodges in an impregnable castle and his army is

97

no smaller than mine. My father once tried to besiege the castle of that rebel but he was compelled to retire from its walls in shame. Ask, gracious lady, all the knights here present and they will bear out my words."

And the knights chimed in a chorus, "Our king speaks the truth. It would be futile to attack Earl Albert of Montclair."

But Godfrey came forward from the midst of the knights, and, blazing with noble anger, said, "Do my ears deceive me, most gracious King, and you honorable sirs? Do you really wish to dismiss this widow with her wrongs unavenged, for fear of a single brigand and rebel? Have you forgotten that it is the first duty of a knight to defend the weak and oppressed?

The king frowned.

"Godfrey," he said, "I esteem you highly and you are as dear to me as my own son. But though you are a great knight, it is unbecoming for you to accuse white-haired men of cowardice. For valor, Godfrey, is one thing and foolhardiness quite another. How shall we have helped this widow if we perish at the walls of Albert's castle?"

"It well behooves a knight," retorted Godfrey, "to perish in the cause of one oppressed rather than to send him off empty-handed."

The knights were very angry and one of them sneered, "Why do you reproach us for not championing this widow? If you are so brave and so true to your knightly duties as to risk death, then champion her yourself. The road to Montclair is open to all. Ride thither and fight then, 'undaunted' knight."

Godfrey made no response, but walked out of the room, and all thought that he was offended or ashamed, having perceived the injustice of his reproaches.

But he was nothing of the sort.

Godfrey went to his quarters and, having thrown off his velvet garments, clad himself from head to toe in mail, whereupon he called his armorbearer and bade him saddle his steed.

"Shall I lead your horse to the main gate, my lord?" his armorbearer asked him.

Godfrey replied, "No, armorbearer, not to the main gate, but to the side one, that nobody may see it."

And the armorbearer asked him further, "Shall I ride along with you, my lord?"

And Godfrey replied, "No, armorbearer, I shall ride alone."

And the armorbearer inquired, "Will you be returning soon, my lord?"

And Godfrey answered, smiling strangely, "No, armorbearer, I shall not return soon; most likely I shall not return ever."

And having mounted his courser, Godfrey rode off toward Montclair. He rode for two days and two nights, and on the third day he stopped before the walls of Earl Albert's castle and blew a trumpet.

A sentinel came out and called, "What do you wish, stranger? Are you come to visit my noble master? Shall I let down the drawbridge?"

But Godfrey replied: "I do not sojourn under the roofs of vile bandits, sentinel. Go to your master and tell him that Godfrey the Conqueror, Knight of the Star of the Nativity, awaits him outside the castle gate. If he restores to the widow of King Sigmund's vassal the property he has stolen, and if he will go, on foot, bareheaded and without his sword, to ask forgiveness of that lady for violence and plunder, and of the king for disobedience, then Godfrey will ride back whence he came. But if he is unwilling to do this, let him come here and engage Godfrey. I challenge him and all his knights."

The sentinel was greatly astonished at Godfrey's boldness but he made no answer and went to repeat Godfrey's words to his lord.

Earl Albert just then was engaged in feasting with his entire troop in the grand hall of the castle. The sentinel presented himself and delivered Godfrey's message. Earl Albert listened in silence and his face turned purple, as if all his blood had surged to his head. His eyes bulged like those of an angry bull, the veins on his forehead swelled and his hand grasped by turns his sword and his throat as if he were afraid of choking with rage.

"Ho!" he roared at length. "Give me my sword and my armor. I will show this arrogant youth what it means to insult the Earl of Montclair."

But the old castle steward shook his head and said:

"Truly, my lord, it would be unreasonable of you to go out and fight this young knight. For what was in King Sigmund's mind when he sent him here? He surely must have thought: If Earl Albert, angered by Godfrey's audacity, has the young knight slain by his servants, I shall broadcast this far and wide and shall disgrace him in the eyes of all Christian knights. But if he goes out and fights Godfrey, then perhaps Earl Albert will succumb and I shall be rid of a rebellious vassal, and shall seize his domains. Or else he might kill Godfrey, whereupon I shall proclaim that he did not slay him in a noble, knightly contest but by treacherously assailing him with his troop from all sides. Everyone will readily believe this, for the young knight enjoys great fame and it is said that there is no one at King Sigmund's court who can stand his ground against him."

Thus spoke the old steward and once again Albert almost choked with rage. He stamped his foot to make the great hall echo.

"What am I to do then?" he shouted. "Must I suffer that insolent youth to revile me with impunity?"

"My lord," replied the steward, "listen to the advice of an old servant. Send a groom and have him tell Godfrey that Earl Albert of Montclair does not cross swords with all comers. Let him go back then whence he came. In this manner you will thwart King Sigmund's cunning and clever scheme and at the same time you will punish Godfrey even more severely than if you had defeated him in combat. For what greater disgrace is there for a knight than contempt?"

Earl Albert was well pleased with this advice and ordered the sentinel to repeat the steward's words to Godfrey.

Godfrey listened to him quietly and said, "Watchman, tell your master that a knight who takes up the cause of a wrongdoer's victim may fall in battle, but will not abandon that cause without combat. Therefore, I shall tarry here till the Earl of Montclair comes out to fight."

Thus having spoken, he stood there erect and motionless, with his drawn sword in his hand, as befitted a knight who had challenged his enemy to mortal combat and awaited his arrival.

Earl Albert laughed aloud when the watchman had returned with Godfrey's answer.

"Let him wait then," he exclaimed. "That does not disturb me in the least. We are enjoying ourselves here, with our glasses."

And Earl Albert reveled with his knights, he reveled all night long and retired only at dawn.

He slept a heavy, deep and long sleep, being dazed with the thick, golden mead and the blood-red wine. And when he awoke the sun was already high in the sky. So he rose from his wide bed that was blanketed with soft skins and went out onto the walls to see that the sentinels were posted and that everyone was doing his duty.

He looked out and saw, down at the gates, a young knight, of handsome stature, erect and motionless, with his drawn sword in his hand. Albert, greatly astonished, inquired of the watchman, "Sentinel, who is that knight and why is he waiting there?"

And the sentinel replied:

"Have you forgotten, my lord, the challenge I repeated to you last evening? That young knight is Godfrey the Conqueror and he is waiting for you, Earl of Montclair. He has stood thus since yesterday, without so much as stirring, in fulfillment of his knightly pledge."

Earl Albert shrugged.

"There is great stubbornness in that youth," he said, "and he is very unreasonable to boot. Does he believe that in this manner he will force me into combat against my will? That is a laughable delusion. Let him stand, if it pleases him, be it till doomsday. Meanwhile, let the grooms bid all my knights to another feast."

And again Albert reveled all day and all night and at dawn he summoned a page and bade him ask the watchman if Godfrey had long since departed.

The page returned after a while and said, "Honorable master, Godfrey has not departed at all. He stands outside the gate, upright and motionless, with his drawn sword in his hand as befits a knight who has challenged an opponent to mortal combat and awaits his arrival."

Earl Albert uttered a curse and, strangely wrathful and sullen, he went to his apartment, where, having bolted the door, he meditated in solitude.

On the evening of that day a frightful storm broke. The oldest men agreed that they had never witnessed such a storm.

The blinding flashes of lightning seemed to tear the sky apart; the crash of the thunder was deafening, and the rain, which came down in torrents, frightened the watchmen from the walls. Everybody sought shelter as best he could and wherever he could. The storm raged all through the night and not until sunrise did it begin to abate.

Then Albert called a page and ordered him to go and ask the steward who lodged in the tower whether Godfrey had not long since departed.

Fairly frightened and wading knee-deep in water, the page reached the tower of the steward and repeated to him the master's query. The steward took him by the hand and, leading him to the window, said briefly, "Behold."

The page looked out and uttered a cry of great astonishment. Godfrey still stood there erect and motionless as he had stood all night amid the flashes of lightnings, the roar of thunder and the pouring rain. His drawn sword was in his hand as befitted a knight who had challenged his opponent to mortal combat and awaited his arrival.

Back to the earl, then, went the page and told what he had seen.

Albert glared at him sulkily and pointed to the door. The page, dismissed, went away, but the servant who remained outside the door to attend his master's call heard how Earl Albert ceaselessly clumped back and forth in his apartment like a ferocious beast trapped in a cage.

On the next day such a heat ensued, following the storm, that it seemed as if molten fire streamed down from the sky. And again the oldest men were saying that within their memory there had been no such heat. No one ventured out of doors, for the hot air scorched the lungs, the stones of the courtyard were like burning embers and the water in the well had dried up.

Earl Albert opened the door of his chamber, climbed up the winding stairs to the tower, and looked out.

Down by the walls of the castle, on top of which not a single watchman remained, in the field that the sun had parched until it was as a sand desert, stood Godfrey. His armor had become so red-hot that it seemed a pillar of fire gleaming with a strange light. He stood erect and motionless, his drawn sword in his hand as befitted a knight who had challenged his opponent to mortal combat and awaited his arrival.

For a long while Earl Albert gazed at him, and there was neither anger nor mockery in the countenance of the Lord of Montclair. He was very pale and his eyes filled with tears.

And suddenly Earl Albert swayed as if an arrow of that knight down there had pierced his very heart.

And the Earl of Montclair fell on his knees, beat his breast and sobbed like a child. Presently he ordered a hairshirt and a coarse sackcloth brought to him and, barefooted and bareheaded, he strode across the drawbridge and stopped before Godfrey.

But Godfrey did not see him.

The knight's face was parched, his mouth cracked from heat and thirst, and his eyes were bloodshot and blinded by the sun.

Albert knelt down before Godfrey, embraced his knees and said, "You have subdued me, Conqueror. Restore to the widow for whose honor you have fought so bravely and tenaciously, as no knight has hitherto, the lands that are rightfully hers, and take my domains and castle for your own as war booty. I am your slave and will do whatever you may command. There is only one favor that I beg of you; enter the castle, which until today I have called mine, and restore and rest yourself."

But Godfrey pressed Albert's head against his breast and responded, "God forbid that I take your domains and your castle away from you. Make right the wrong you have done, and be a friend to me, and I shall gladly enter your house and rest therein."

Thus they entered the castle together and Earl Albert, having treated his guest, helped him into a bed of soft skins, and watched over him till morn.

On the morrow Godfrey awoke hale and rested, and made his departure.

But the fame of his deed had sped before him, and, when he reached the castle there awaited him outside the gate the most gracious king himself and Princess, Roxana, as well as the whole court and all the vassals.

Godfrey dismounted to greet the king, but the king said, "Hail to you, Godfrey the Conqueror. From this day we shall call you not only 'Conqueror,' but 'Indomitable' as well." And then, ungirding his sword, he added, "I am already too old to mete justice and lead my knights into battle, and God has given me no son. Hereafter you shall be the leader of my army. Here is my sword as an emblem of your authority."

And the knights concurred.

"The choice is just, in sooth, for though there are many amongst us who are his elders there is none who is worthier."

Godfrey took, then, the sword from the royal hands and girded himself with it while the knights formed a circle around him.

But Godfrey looked beyond them to Princess Roxana who stood beside the king and smiled at him with the loveliest of her smiles.

Tale 9

¶ *The Princess of the Seas shall present him with a magic ring that shall give him power over the ocean.*

AVE you ever seen dead stones, noble sirs?

Have you ever set eyes on pearls lying in a deep swoon without luster, on sapphires that have lost their blue, on emeralds that no longer shimmer with the green of the sea, on rubies that no longer glow with a blood-red, mysterious light, on opals no longer iridescent like the rainbow?

Have you ever seen dead stones, noble sirs?

I do not ask you out of idle curiosity. I want to warn you lest you ever restore such stones to life. Above all, however, I want to advise you that, if you ever hear of a man who restores such stones, you should not trust him, and should shun his house and avoid meeting him on any road, by day or by night.

Listen to this tale and you will be convinced that my counsel is right and wise, and many hidden things will become clear and intelligible to you.

Listen to this tale of a dreadful and mysterious occurrence. It came to pass at King Sigmund's court soon after Godfrey had assumed the leadership of the castle troop.

Having conducted Godfrey through the whole cas-

tle and its ramparts and towers and having shown
him the underground dungeons and the sundry re-
cesses, the king said to him, "You have now seen
everything, my son, save the treasury vault. Let us
go down there now because you must know it as from
now on you will watch over the treasury."

They went down and the servants walked ahead of
them, lighting their way with torches.

At the sight of the king the guards drew apart to
make way for him, but they barred the way to Godfrey with their halberds.

"This knight, called Godfrey the Conqueror, is from
now on your leader and you owe to him obedience as
much as to me," said the king.

With these words, he handed to Godfrey a golden
key and in the presence of the guards bade him open
the door of the treasury, thereby signifying that by
royal authority this thenceforth would be his right.
Whereupon they both entered the underground
chambers of the treasury.

Godfrey marveled at the immense coffers filled to
the brim with silver, gold and precious stones, at the
diverse armor expertly forged from precious metals,
at the raiments of gold and silver brocade, delicately

embroidered and glittering with jewels, at the precious furs from the far north and the soft and richly patterned carpets from the Orient.

But while marveling at all this, he did not forget to look about intently, marking carefully how the chambers and the passageways were disposed, where the caches and the secret passages were and how they were opened. The king highly praised his agility and rejoiced inwardly at having made so wise a choice in appointing Godfrey the leader.

As they went together from one chamber to another, Godfrey stopped abruptly and gazed attentively at one of the walls. Surprised, the king inquired:

"Tell me, Godfrey, why do you peer at this old wall so intently? You did not admire my finest jewels so long."

"Most gracious lord," answered Godfrey, "do you not see that along this wall there run cracks so clear and plain that they have been made with some purpose, and that they form the outline of a door?"

"There are many such fissures in the old walls of my castle and they often form the queerest designs," said the king, shrugging his shoulders.

But Godfrey went up to the wall and, laying his hands on the door so marked, pushed it with all his strength.

Slowly the wall opened, revealing a dark passageway leading to the underground depths.

"Godfrey," exclaimed the amazed king, "you have uncovered secret passages of which not only I, but my father and grandfather knew nothing. Truly, nothing can remain concealed from your eyes."

The king groped his way down the stone steps, with Godfrey following. Soon they came to a tightly bolted iron door, and opening it they found themselves in a small, low-vaulted, dark room in the center of which stood a huge bronze chest.

"Undoubtedly," said the king, "we shall find here the most priceless jewels of the treasury, if my grandfather or my great-grandfather hid them so secretly and so artfully."

When, however, Godfrey lifted the heavy lid of the chest, they discovered but three necklaces—one of pearls, another of emeralds, and a third of opals. True, the three necklaces were very delicately fashioned and the stones in them were of unusual size, but of what use were they, for all the jewels had lost their brilliance and color. They were stones long since dead.

King Sigmund, however, viewed them with joy and delight.

"Here are jewels worthy of my daughter, Princess Roxana," he cried. "Godfrey, have them sent to my alchemist. He will restore to them the brilliance they have lost."

The alchemist, however, on hearing the royal desire replied, "I cannot restore life to these stones. It is not in my power to do so any more than it is in my power to resurrect the dead."

And then a strange thing came to pass. King Sigmund, who ordinarily cared not much for jewels, became obsessed with a sudden and irrepressible craving for these stones as they were formerly, alive, glistening with the colors of the rainbow, marvelously beautiful. All other affairs ceased to concern him. No longer did he go to hunt, nor did he build strongholds, he went on war raids no more, nor did he feast with his knights. He dispatched messengers to all corners of the earth, offering great rewards to him who would bring life to the dead stones. And to his castle he invited all merchants who were returning from overseas, that he might question them at great length to learn if they had not heard of such a sage.

All in vain, however.

And the king grew ever more melancholy and dispirited.

In vain did his faithful subjects, desiring to cheer his heart, bring him the finest jewels. The king yearned only for those that were dead. This odd and unaccountable yearning grew stronger from day to day, so much so that one day King Sigmund, heretofore noted for his piety and Christian virtues, said to Godfrey in the presence of all knights:

"Your efforts to solace me, Godfrey, are useless. I feel that I shall die of sorrow if I fail to revive these stones. Were the evil spirit himself to appear here to restore them, I should accept his aid without hesitation."

Oh, how thoughtless and rash were these words! And how soon the king was to atone for them.

That same night such a furious storm broke over the castle that nobody retired for the night.

The servants gathered in the servants' hall, the court ladies in Princess Roxana's apartments and the knights in the large castle hall, and everybody whiled away his time as best he could—for, as is well known, one is more cheerful in company than alone.

King Sigmund was seated before an immense fire that had been kindled in the hearth. He was deep in brooding thought.

Unlike most of his knights, he did not indulge in drinking, he did not watch the game of dice, nor did he listen to the tales and ballads which a bard sang for the pleasure of the assembled knights. In that large and noisy hall the king appeared to be quite lonely.

Meanwhile the storm raged hour after hour.

Toward midnight the blast of a trumpet was heard suddenly, then the voice of someone calling as if he strove to make himself heard above the howling of the wind and the crash of thunder. Finally there was the clangor of the drawbridge chains as the bridge was lowered apparently by the castle guards.

There was great surprise among the knights. Who could be arriving at the castle at that time of the night and in such a storm? A feeling of vague uneasiness fell on the gathering.

After a short while a strangely pale and bewildered page came into the hall and, bowing to the king, addressed him in these words:

"Most gracious lord, a man describing himself as a restorer of dead stones desires to see you. But I think he should be sent away from here at once, and the guards ordered never again to let him enter."

King Sigmund, however, took no notice of the page's ashen face or of his words.

"Show him in forthwith," the king exclaimed, and rose with unwonted briskness as if to go out and meet the stranger.

For a moment the page wavered, apparently desiring to say something more, but observing the king's impatience he went out and presently returned with the visitor.

No sooner had the stranger entered the hall, than all felt their vague troubled uneasiness transformed to an eerie and uncontrollable terror.

In appearance the visitor was a tall, white-haired old man of grave, even respectable, mien. And yet there was something peculiar in his manner, something suggestive of a slinking beast. And his eyes. Were they not those of a lurking tiger? Strange green eyes without pupils and whites, eyes like two green lanterns with red flames burning inside.

King Sigmund, however, was not disturbed and greeted the visitor heartily and joyfully as a long-awaited guest.

"You are the restorer of dead stones?" he inquired, bidding the visitor sit by his side.

"Yes, most gracious lord," answered the stranger. "It came to my notice that you possess stones which you wish to revive and here I am at your service."

"Master," declared the king, overjoyed, "if you really succeed in accomplishing this, there is nothing I will refuse you. You shall have as a reward all the silver and gold that you may demand, and over and above this I will accord you my royal friendship and favor."

Thus he spoke and the stranger bowed humbly, at the same time smiling mockingly. The smile made Godfrey's blood boil, but King Sigmund did not or would not see anything amiss. He ordered Godfrey to give the jewels to the visitor, who then politely took his leave.

Some three days passed. Then, again there was a knocking on the castle gate at midnight. This time the visitor was not the restorer of dead stones but his servant, a little black dwarf. He was bringing back the necklaces to the king. When the king opened the small bronze casket where the jewels were lodged a shout of joy burst from his throat. For surely nobody ever had seen such superb jewels.

The green of the emeralds was strangely deep and limpid.

The pearls gleamed with the faint, rosy-gold light of dawn.

The rubies glowed with the hot crimson of fire.

The king ordered that a sackful of gold should be given to the dwarf and, having called Princess Roxana, he presented her with the three necklaces, enjoining her to wear one of them at all times.

On the following day, however, Princess Roxana came out of her room very pale and sad.

"Father and my king," she said, "I will not wear these jewels. Tell the treasurer to take them away. I had a strange dream last night. I dreamed that the emeralds of my necklace were beginning to move slowly as though they were alive, to nudge one another and tap this song:

"Bright and limpid
Is our green,
Like naiads' eyes
That you've seen.

"Then they began to wind around me like a long green snake and, coming closer and closer, they wound their cold, slippery coils about my neck and breast. I awoke trembling all over my body, and felt weak, almost ill."

Thus spoke the princess, but the king shrugged his shoulders.

"Dreams are sometimes very strange," he said. "But that is no reason for giving up such beautiful jewels."

And he ordered his troubadours to entertain the princess with merry songs.

On the following day, however, the princess rose from bed even sadder and paler.

"Father," she said, "today I had a dream that was even stranger than the last. I dreamed that the pearls of my necklace began to spin above my head like a swarm of golden fireflies, singing thus:

"With rosy gold
We gleam and gleam,
Pampered by water nymphs
In their lonely dream.

"The song was so moving and plaintive that when I awoke my pillow was wet with tears. No, I will not wear these jewels again."

"Dreams are sometimes sad and sometimes cheerful, Roxana," answered the king, smiling, "but you should not think of them once they are gone. A dream is like autumn fog. Who thinks of dreary days when the sun shines?"

And in order to cheer the princess he ordered that preparations should be made for a great feast.

On the next day, however, Princess Roxana did not rise from bed at all and in vain did the alarmed physicians endeavor to restore her strength. The dream that had visited her the night before had so terrified her that she was taken gravely ill.

She had dreamed that the rubies of her necklace began to soar, sparkling ever more intensely, and then dropped heavily like large crimson drops of blood, striking one another and tapping this song:

We sparkle and sparkle
With crimson and fire,
For 'tis young blood
Colors our attire.

And then the emeralds and the pearls began to soar
along with them, and drop and spin and dance some
strange dance, tapping a wild and eerie tune which
sounded by turns like weeping and like laughter.

Now the king was greatly saddened and frightened
but although he ordered the jewels locked away in
the vault, the strange dreams not only continued to
afflict the princess, but also began to haunt the king
and his knights.

At night it seemed to all of them that they heard a
gentle ringing on the stairs leading from the treasury:
it was the stones coming from the underground vault
in a long rainbow-colored procession and running up
into the royal chambers.

The terror-stricken king ordered the jewels to be
locked up in an iron chest and thrown into the near-by
lake.

But it was not so easy, gentle sirs, to do away with
those charmed stones.

That same night the fishermen who lived above the lake heard the ringing of strange little bells.

It must be the water nymphs driving their goats to the lea by the lake, they thought, and gripped by curiosity they leaned gingerly out of their huts to catch a glimpse of those water flocks. But it was not water goats.

It was the charmed stones that rose from the depths of the lake and, sparkling with magnificent colors, swiftly made their way toward the royal castle.

Such a terror descended upon the castle that as soon as dusk fell nobody dared remain in his own chamber, and the guards took refuge in the servants' hall whenever they perceived the slightest murmur.

In vain did Godfrey endeavor to uphold their courage. In vain did he rage at them or try to shame them. The bravest soldiers would answer him that they were ever ready to confront a foe but not charms and evil spirits.

Princess Roxana, however, suffered most of all because the bad dreams visited her most often and with the greatest persistence. Hence her illness made alarming progress, and the physicians began to fear for her life.

128

The poor king spent whole days at the bedside of his beloved daughter on whose head he had himself brought down such ill-luck. And Godfrey, noting how his most beloved maiden grew weaker day by day, helplessly clenched his fists, not knowing how to save her. One night, however, he suddenly recalled what had been reported by the castle servants—namely, that the dwarf who had brought the jewels from the restorer of dead stones had been unable to carry by himself the sack of gold bestowed by the king and that he had asked the help of one of the servants. This servant, then, must know where the restorer of dead stones dwelt. And who but that magician could have cast a spell on the royal jewels? Therefore, losing not a moment of time, Godfrey rose from his bed, ordered his armorbearer to fetch his sword and armor, and to summon that servant to be his guide.

The house of the restorer of dead stones stood far from the castle in a complete wilderness, and was surrounded by a high wall. But in vain did Godfrey search for some gate in this wall in order to knock for admittance. There was no gate of any kind, nor any opening. It appeared that nobody ever entered or went out of that place.

"Did you not see how the dwarf got in?" Godfrey asked the servant.

"No, sir," replied the servant. "As soon as we came to the wall he gave me a gold coin and told me to be gone, which I willingly did. For, to speak the truth, I liked that little black devil even less than his master and I was happy when I found myself safe and sound in the castle."

Evidently this wall opens only at the sound of a magic word, thought Godfrey. But this is too small an obstacle to hold me back. And without another thought he tied his horse to a tree and proceeded to climb the wall, now grasping the bricks that protruded here and there, now gripping the wild creeping vines which covered the wall. And as he had once learned from his fellow-shepherds to climb up inaccessible rocks and cliffs, he reached the top of the wall in a trice.

The night was clear even though the moving clouds now and then screened the moon, so Godfrey could plainly see from this height the sorcerer's home and the wild, weedy garden that enclosed it. And a weird house it was: all of black granite, with no windows or doors. It had the appearance of a mighty, smoothly

130

hewn block rather than of someone's habitation.

Suddenly, in the deep stillness of the night, un-ruffled even by the sound of leaves stirring in the wind, Godfrey heard a peculiar murmur coming from somewhere deep in the garden. It sounded like the noise of the sea, or like soft weeping, or like the distant moaning of the wind.

Godfrey grasped the branch of a large pine tree that grew close to the wall, climbed down to the ground and proceeded in the direction whence the sound came. He did not search long. He had walked but a few steps when he spied among the trees a young girl who was weeping in this peculiar, anguished way. Her long green hair enfolded her as if in a cloak and large tears trickled between the fingers of her tiny white hands with which she covered her face.

"Who are you and can I help you?" inquired Godfrey.

The girl looked up, and Godfrey observed that her eyes were green as the sea, her face lucent as alabaster and her whole body covered with scales of precious stones that shimmered with all the colors of the rainbow.

"How did you enter here, knight?" she said. "Be off, be off at once if you cherish your life. The sorcerer will be here anon and then it will be too late."

"'Tis truly not my habit to flee a foe," Godfrey replied, smiling. "Tell me rather who has wronged you that you cry so pitifully, and be assured that I shall defend you and shall shirk no foe."

"No foe? That may be so, knight, but it is not an enemy who will come, it is a monster without fangs or muzzle, a monster like a giant octopus, a monster who overpowers all with the fascinating green light of his eyes that attract and devour. If you truly wish to help me instead of perishing uselessly and gruesomely, climb up that tree quickly, that he may not see you. But bind yourself fast to it with your knight's belt."

Godfrey complied with her wish. He had scarcely done so when he sighted the restorer of dead stones approaching, followed by his dwarf who carried a large iron chest. The dwarf set down the chest, lifted its lid and handed to his master a small crystal wand. With this wand the sorcerer drew a wide circle about him, whereupon he said to the green-haired maiden,

"Daughter of the King of the Sea, daughter of the King of the Sea, will you freely feed my stones with your blood and your yearning and your tears?"

The maiden rose to her feet and regarded him proudly.

"No, you vile monster," she retorted. "Never will Princess Lilian aid you in your accursed tricks. You may take my blood and tears by force, but you shall not make a willing slave of me."

No sooner had she spoken these words than the body of the sorcerer began to change shape and color and finally dissolved into a large jelly-like mass, with thousands of popping and retracting tentacles in the middle of which a single terrifying eye glared with a peculiar green light.

And as Godfrey gazed at that light a great impotence and weakness overcame him so that he was unable to draw his sword, while at the same time some irresistible force seemed to pull him toward the monster. Had he not fastened himself to the tree with his belt he would surely have climbed down and perished miserably.

Meanwhile the monster glowered at the maiden,

133

and she, under the influence of the mute command of his stare, slowly raised her hands aloft and stood there motionless like a statue.

And then the brilliant stones which swathed all her body fell from off her, string by string, and like a snake of a thousand hues began to return to the chest, while at the same time there issued from the chest another snake of precious, but lusterless and colorless stones which crept up to her and began slowly to coil round her body.

Godfrey closed his eyes to shut out the sight and when he opened them neither the restorer of dead stones nor his dwarf was there.

Then only did he recover his strength and his senses.

He unfastened his belt, slid down the tree and, drawing his sword, was about to run after them. But he was stopped by the voice of the water nymph:

"What are you doing? Have you lost your mind? Did you not realize a while ago that you are powerless against him? If you truly wish to help me, listen to my advice."

Godfrey halted, and the green-haired maiden commenced her tale.

"I am the daughter of the King of the Sea and my name is Lilian. That monster of a sorcerer once lured me ashore and carried me off, that he might feed his stones with my blood, tears and longing. Look how the emeralds, rubies, pearls and amethysts on my body begin to come to life and brilliance. I cannot escape from here even though I am unguarded, because these stones take away all my strength and only the sorcerer's magic word can remove them from my body. Therefore, if you want to defeat him, go to the seashore and call three times: 'King of the Sea, in your daughter's name I summon you.' My father will then appear before you, and when you tell him of my ill-fortune, he will give you the flower of a charmed seaweed. Then, if you can approach the sorcerer unnoticed and touch him with that flower, the fiend will lose his magic power and you will be able to overcome him. Remember, however, that if he hears the sound of your steps before you touch him with the magic flower, you will be done for. Are you not afraid?"

Godfrey did not even reply. He climbed over the wall, swung himself on his horse and galloped off toward the sea.

137

He rode for two days and two nights, stopping only long enough to give his horse a rest and restore himself, and on the third day he reached the seashore. The sea that day was calm and still and the sky seemed to lend its blue to the water. But when Godfrey, having set foot upon the golden sand, had thrice called upon the King of the Sea, a wind suddenly rose, the sky clouded and the waves turned green and foaming.

Yet instead of swelling up with a threatening roar and crashing defiantly against the shore and then receding, as waves do before a storm, they were transformed into a large silver-scaled snake. Lifting up its head, which was topped with a glittering golden crown, the snake inquired of Godfrey, "You who have summoned me in my daughter's name, what is your wish and what tidings do you bear me from her?"

"I wish for the flower of the charmed seaweed," answered Godfrey, "and I bring you sad tidings from her. She is held captive by a cruel monster called the restorer of dead stones. Yet do not despair, King of the Sea. God grant that with the aid of that wonder flower I may set her free."

The King of the Sea whistled long and low.

At this whistle a water nymph, her head wreathed with starfish, rose from beneath the water and, bowing to the king, said, "My king and ruler of the waters, here I am at your command. Shall I cast a spell on ships? Shall I search for pearls in the green depths? Shall I fetch many-colored shells from afar, or wreaths of water lilies or of coral?"

The king replied, "In my garden, guarded by snakes, grows a wondrous flower, differing from all others. Fetch me the flower of the charmed seaweed, water nymph, the flower that spells death, the fiery wonder of the sea."

The nymph vanished in the waves and after a while emerged again holding in her hand the magic flower which sent forth wondrous fiery and purple flashes.

No sooner had Godfrey taken it into his hand than the sky cleared, the wind subsided, and the sea turned blue. The king and the water nymph were gone so Godfrey remounted his courser and set off on his return journey.

Once more it was the dead of night when he reached the wall which surrounded the sorcerer's dwelling. He entered the garden in the same manner as before. Princess Lilian, though pale and anxious, greeted her savior with joy.

"You have come in the nick of time, Godfrey," she said. "The sorcerer is now teaching his stones the witch dance with which they torment people afterward and he is usually so engrossed in this occupation that he pays no attention to what goes on around him, so it will be fairly easy for you to approach him unnoticed. He is in his house, the walls of which will move apart the instant you touch them with the magic flower. Go, then, and may God help you in this struggle."

Godfrey drew his sword and when he came to the house he touched its walls with the flower of the seaweed. The walls moved apart noiselessly and Godfrey entered.

He passed through several halls illumined with a red light that seemed to come from nowhere, their walls painted with curious arabesques of magic signs. At length, Godfrey found himself in a room from which came the music of a flute that he had already heard from afar. In the center of the room burned a fire whose flame kept changing from purple to green, then to yellow and then to violet. In its flickering light Godfrey saw the black dwarf who squatted by the fire and played a small golden flute. Behind the dwarf stood the sorcerer who was making strange signs with the crystal wand which Godfrey had already seen in the garden.

It seemed that the tempo of the dwarf's music followed exactly the motions of the sorcerer's wand, and in the very same rhythm the precious stones rose like a shower of colored sparks from the chests standing by the walls and then dropped back with a gentle ring.

And so engrossed was the sorcerer that, as Princess Lilian had predicted, he was unaware of Godfrey's approach and turned only when Godfrey had touched him with the flower of the seaweed.

The monster roared with rage and, drawing his sword, set upon Godfrey. But there was as yet no match for the "Conqueror." And it was not long before the restorer of dead stones lay dead at Godfrey's feet.

Godfrey ran into the garden to announce the glad tidings to the Princess of the Sea, but he found that she already was free of the baneful spell.

"Godfrey," she called, "I wish you to know that from now on my father and I are your most faithful friends. Take this ring as a token from the Princess of the Sea."

Godfrey bade her farewell and set out for the castle, where Princess Roxana, now recovered, and the whole court impatiently awaited him.

But he did not know that the ring which he had received from Princess Lilian vested in him secret power over the sea.

𝕿ale 10

℄ *Vivian the Sorceress shall bestow upon him an amethyst of miraculous and mysterious power.*

T was an old custom of the knights at King Sigmund's court while indulging themselves with wine to praise the graces of their ladies and discourse upon the deeds which each of them was ready to perform in honor of his lady. It was a diversion much affected by the knights and each one strove to outdo his companions in his boasting.

On such occasions, too, there was much merrymaking, gentle sirs, and not one of them would yield to the other in knightly courage and fancy.

Thus Earl Arthur, surnamed "the Impetuous," said: "My lady is Blanche of the radiant eyes, and in her honor I stand ready to challenge and defeat seven knights, engaging them not one at a time but all at once."

"The deed would be none too great—indeed, too small to honor my lady, Yolanda, of the silver voice and the white hands," instantly replied John, a young and courtly knight called "the Handsome" for his graceful figure. "As for me, I am ready to honor my lady by crossing the Sea Monsters' bay alone in a fishing boat, and you all know that even the largest and sturdiest craft will not venture into that bay. More than that, I am willing to swim across the bay, regardless of its whirlpools, its great depth, its sea monsters."

Thus the knights vied with each other in their boasts.

Godfrey alone kept silent. So King Sigmund, who had been listening with a kindly smile to the fancies of his knights, inquired:

"And you, Godfrey, what deed would you be ready to perform in honor of my daughter, Princess Roxana?"

"I am thinking of that, most gracious lord," said Godfrey, "but I can find nothing worthy of my golden-haired mistress. Unless for her sake I go in quest of the charmed amethyst flower."

"What is this charmed amethyst flower?" asked the king in surprise. "I have never heard of it."

"Is that possible, sire?" said Godfrey. "The flower grows within the confines of your realm on a high mountain called 'the Inaccessible.' It was planted there by the King of the Mountains who surrounded it with a ring of fire, over which his daughter Vivian stands guard. Only that knight can pluck it who will

146

pass fearlessly through the fire. But should his heart tremble even for a fleeting moment while he steps into the fire, he will be burned to ashes."

"I, too, have heard of that flower," said the old castle steward. "Its stem is of gold, its petals have the color and luster of an amethyst, and its leaves glisten with all the colors of the rainbow. That flower, more-over, possesses magic power; he who holds it can understand the language of flowers, trees and birds, can with one touch restore health to the infirm, make the ugly beautiful and turn old men into youths. It is truly a beautiful deed that Godfrey has conceived as homage to our princess."

But Arnold of Treville, who never could forgive Godfrey the defeat which Godfrey, while still a boy, had inflicted upon him in the presence of the king and all the knights, and who now, as was his habit, had been drinking to excess, laughed coarsely and began to sneer at Godfrey:

"The steward has spoken the truth in saying that Godfrey has conceived a beautiful deed to honor his lady. But it is just as true that it is easier to brag while drinking than to execute what has been promised."

Godfrey turned pale with anger, while King Sigmund said to Arnold, "Your words, Earl Arnold, are improper and quite injudicious. It is common knowledge that Godfrey the Conqueror has a stout and intrepid heart. Therefore, even if he has exaggerated somewhat in offering my daughter a deed that no man is able to accomplish (for who will not tremble ever so briefly when stepping into flames?) he proposed it in order to show his esteem and affection for her. Besides, other knights likewise have boasted here of deeds which it is not in their power to perform, and this sport is no more than bragging."

But Arnold of Treville, quaffing the golden mead from a large pewter, though, as I said, he had long since had his full measure, replied to the king in these terms:

"Gracious King, I well know that this sport is merely bragging, but, ha, ha, even boasts have their limits. Otherwise, why should Godfrey not say: 'I will uproot the tallest pine tree that grows in the castle grounds; I will bend one end of it into a hook, set two mountains one on top of the other and, climbing on them, I will take down the moon with this pole and offer it to the princess that she may wear it

148

as a medallion on a golden chain.' Ha, ha, that would be some deed, truly worthy of Princess Roxana!"

The knights could not restrain their mirth and the king himself laughed aloud. But Godfrey, unaccustomed to being sneered at and jested with, flared up in anger and, rising from the table, said, "You are mistaken, Earl Arnold, in regarding my words as an idle boast. You are mistaken, and I wish you to know that I am setting out straightaway for the Inaccessible Mountain and I shall either perish or bring back to the princess the magic amethyst flower."

The king, frightened at the unfortunate turn the matter was taking, said, "You are about to act unwisely, Godfrey, by endangering your life for the sake of an idle boast. It is one thing to risk one's head in defense of someone who is oppressed, and quite another to do so for a senseless boast."

And Godfrey would have calmed down and refrained from carrying out his intention, for at heart he felt that the king was right, had Arnold of Treville not spoken.

"Gracious lord, let him go to that mountain and let him not forget to take that pine tree with him so that he can take down, ha, ha, the moon while there."

This time the king's pleading and reasoning were of no avail. Godfrey would listen to no one, and, wishing to put an end to the idle talk, he said, "I vow by my word as a knight that before the day is out I will set forth from the castle and if I do not perish, I will bring to the princess the amethyst flower."

No longer could anyone restrain him, for a knight's pledge is a sacred thing and he who does not keep it lays himself open to scorn and derision. Godfrey took leave of the assembled knights. King Sigmund hugged Godfrey's head to his breast.

"I desire you to know, Godfrey, that I have long meant to betroth to you my daughter and to make you my successor. If, then, you come back alive you shall receive the princess' hand in return for the amethyst flower."

Godfrey was overjoyed. "Gracious King, even if that flower is surrounded not with one, but with a hundred rings of fire, I shall return safe and sound," he exclaimed. "For how can my courage fail me if I know that I am to receive such a reward?"

Setting off in great haste, he soon found himself at the foot of the Inaccessible Mountain.

Boldly and cheerfully Godfrey began to climb,

thinking of the not distant future when, on his victorious return to the castle, he would receive the hand of his beloved.

Boldly and cheerfully he surveyed the wreath of awesome fire which encircled the magic flower and he strode into it without a qualm.

The flames parted before him and Godfrey beheld the marvelous amethyst flower. In silence and great admiration the knight contemplated it for a long while and then he reached out to pluck it.

At that very moment, however, he felt someone touch his arm and he turned around.

Before him stood a lovely lady with amethyst-colored eyes. She was clad in a light, flowing robe, and at her shoulders were rainbow-colored wings. She looked at him imploringly.

"Godfrey," she begged, "I entreat you, do not touch that flower. It is the flower of my life, and my father surrounded it with a wreath of flames in order to guard me against danger. If you pluck it, I shall have to die."

"Fair lady," replied Godfrey, greatly moved, "you may rest assured I will not touch this flower. I shall return from whence I came and neither King Sigmund nor Princess Roxana will bear me malice if I come back empty-handed when I tell them what I have heard from you."

"Alas, noble knight," said the mountain princess, "if you tell them the reason why you did not pluck this flower, I shall have to die just as if you had plucked it. You should know that if there be a knight who succeeds in passing through the ring of fire that guards the amethyst flower, I must not ask a favor of him, and if Marlina the Sorceress, queen of all sorceresses, learns that I did so, I shall have to die. Your sacrifice, Godfrey, must remain a secret to all. Tell the king and Roxana that you returned empty-handed because at the sight of the wreath of dreadful flames you did not dare enter it."

"You do not mean that!" exclaimed Godfrey. "I, a knight who is called invincible and indomitable, am to accuse myself of such paltry cowardice? I, Godfrey the Conqueror, am to confess in front of the knights that I broke my word? Why, I should become the laughingstock of all knights for all time to come. Do you not understand, Vivian, that I cannot do what you ask?"

"True," replied Vivian softly, "you cannot do it.

152

For what would become of your glory as a knight? No, I have no right to demand such a sacrifice of you. Pluck, then, this flower that you have won. I see that I must die."

But Godfrey stood motionless, pondering deeply.

"No, Vivian," he said at length, "I will not pluck this flower. If I were to pluck it, I should commit a base act unworthy of a true knight."

"But if you do not pluck it," said Vivian, "everyone will call you a coward."

"Yes," whispered Godfrey, then at once he straightened up proudly and added, "But what of it, Vivian? Am I to fear taunts and jeers? To avoid being called a coward shall I become one in truth? Shall I sacrifice your life for an idle boast and commit a ghastly crime? No, truly, I will not do it."

"And Roxana?" said the Princess of the Mountains. "What will Roxana think of you?"

"Roxana," repeated Godfrey, "Roxana . . . It is true . . . I had almost forgotten about her. She will turn from me with contempt as from a base coward. Vivian, Vivian, I cannot do what you ask. I should prefer a hundred times to die rather than lose her."

"You see, then, that I am right, Godfrey. Hesitate

153

no more. Take my ring in return for this flower, and may you be happy. I myself shall pluck it for you."

And she reached for the magic flower, but Godfrey held back her hand.

"I could not be happy, Vivian," he declared, "knowing that you paid for my happiness with your life. I could never look into Roxana's eyes knowing I had won her at the price of a crime. I would rather she despised me unjustly than that she should have a right to despise me. Farewell, Vivian."

"Farewell, Godfrey," said Vivian, seeing that Godfrey's resolve was unalterable. "I shall never forget that you saved my life. Take this ring from the Princess of the Mountains who loves you like a brother and remember that you have forever a sister and a friend."

Godfrey took from her hand the golden ring with the amethyst but while putting it on his finger he reflected, I wish I had never possessed you for through you I have forfeited a ring that is a hundred times more precious, the ring that was to have been given me by my beloved lady, Princess Roxana.

But not a word did he say aloud for he would not

wound Vivian's heart with vain laments and, having thanked her for her gift, he started homeward.

When the guards who kept watch in the tower of King Sigmund's castle sighted Godfrey nearing the castle, they sent word to the king and Princess Roxana who were awaiting him in great anxiety and alarm. The king, overjoyed, bade all his vassals assemble in the great throne room. There, having settled on his royal throne, he addressed them thus: "Noble sirs, Godfrey the Conqueror will arrive here shortly. It is my desire that we welcome him appropriately and that in the presence of us all he receive from the hands of my daughter his reward for the magic flower which he won by passing through the wreath of fearful flames."

"We do not know yet whether Godfrey has won the amethyst flower or whether he is returning empty-handed," muttered Arnold of Treville.

Although he had not dared to utter these words very loud, the knights who stood nearest to him heard them and rebuked him severely.

"It is anger and envy that blind you, Arnold, and prompt these words," they chided. "For well you know that although none of us would have gone for this flower, Godfrey, having pledged his word as a knight, would die rather than return empty-handed. How dare you, then, suspect Godfrey the Conqueror of cowardice?"

Arnold was shamed and turned silent.

At that very moment the pages opened the wide portals of the throne room and Godfrey appeared. But he did not enter proudly and with his head high as befits a conqueror. He was sad and pale, his head was lowered, and he dared not raise his eyes to the king and the princess who greeted him with beaming smiles.

"Welcome, Godfrey," said the king. "Welcome, indomitable and intrepid knight. I see there is no power capable of besting you, and your heart knows no fear or terror. Present to my daughter the gift you have won for her, and you, Roxana, deliver to him your betrothal ring."

Thus spoke King Sigmund, but Godfrey remained sad and silent, raising his eyes to no one, as if he had not heard the king's words.

The king was astonished.

"What is the meaning of all this, Godfrey?" he

demanded. "Are you not pleased with the reward that awaits you? Does the charmed amethyst flower perchance not grow on the Inaccessible Mountain?"

Godfrey replied, "I cherish this reward above my life, and the charmed amethyst flower does grow on the Inaccessible Mountain as of old. But I have not obtained that flower, sire, and have no right to Princess Roxana's ring."

On hearing this King Sigmund was even more surprised.

"Why is it, then, Godfrey, that you have returned empty-handed? What hindrance checked you?"

Godfrey's head sank even lower; for a moment he hesitated as though the words he was about to utter refused to pass through his throat, and then he answered in a low voice, "Most gracious King, when I laid eyes upon the wreath of huge flames blazing around the charmed flower my heart failed within me, I became aware of the audacity of my undertaking, and shrinking from a horrible death, I departed empty-handed."

The knights gazed at one another in deep amazement.

Had they heard aright? Was it Godfrey the Conqueror who uttered those disgraceful words unworthy of any knight?

Had it been someone else, he would have been greeted with laughter and jeers, he would have been given a distaff and a spindle and he would have been expelled from the ranks of knights. But Godfrey's fame was so great that they all stood speechless and dumfounded and were seized with a strange shame. The ignominy of the most renowned knight among them so affected them that it seemed a reflection upon the honor of the entire company. Even Arnold of Treville dared not laugh or sneer, but kept sullenly silent. King Sigmund whom Godfrey's act offended doubly, not only because he was the leader of the king's company of knights but also the royal Princess' knight, uttered not a word. And such a silence reigned in that immense and well-filled hall that it seemed as if nobody were there.

Godfrey grew paler, for the silence was more oppressive than laughter and scornful words, and he felt alone and forlorn as though he were in some wilderness, not among companions who until now had been his friends.

Suddenly, in the midst of this dead silence, there

resounded the clear ringing voice of Princess Roxana, the king's daughter.

"Truly, Godfrey, I do not believe you," she declared.

All the knights shuddered and directed their eyes toward the dais where Princess Roxana sat beside her father's throne. Godfrey trembled as he gazed at the face of his beloved for the first time since his arrival.

The princess repeated, "Truly, I do not believe you. I do not know why you have returned without the amethyst flower but I do know that abject cowardice is not the reason. I do not demand that you explain your conduct for I see that you cannot do so. I love you and I trust you and my ring belongs to you."

Godfrey took a few steps toward the Princess, sank at her feet, and laying his head on her knees wept like a child.

And Roxana said to him:

"Small-hearted are those who believe the first accusation cast upon a friend even if it comes out of his own mouth. Have you not been their companion in countless raids, the most valiant companion of all? Have you not performed exploits more renowned than any knight can boast of? And yet they have readily believed in your disgrace and have condemned you in their hearts."

And the knights were deeply shamed. How could they even for a moment have imputed to Godfrey such wretched cowardice? Ought they not to have understood that there was some secret that sealed Godfrey's lips? Should they not have greeted with laughter the accusation that he had cast upon himself and trusted their dear companion without so much as inquiring the cause of his ill-success? And the knights surrounded Godfrey, taking him into their arms and pressing his hands, and they began to protest their undying friendship.

Suddenly a strange, rainbow-colored light illumined the great hall, and when the astonished knights turned to see whence this wonderful brightness came, they beheld before them a golden-haired maiden with amethyst-colored eyes and rainbow-tinted wings at her shoulders. In her hand she held the flower.

"I did not want you to suffer too long, Godfrey," said the maiden, smiling upon Godfrey and Roxana, "and I have come to tell your companions and Princess Roxana of your chivalrous deed. But I see that sorceress' witness is needless to him who has won Princess Roxana's loving and trusting heart. Hear me nevertheless, King Sigmund, Princess and ye noble knights, for I desire that Godfrey's deed may be known and everlastingly remembered by all. I am Vivian, the Princess of the Mountains, and my father planted on the Inaccessible Mountain the wondrous amethyst flower. He wished that this flower might come into the possession not only of the bravest but also of the noblest knight. Therefore he ordered me to prove the stout-hearted knight who came through the wreath of flames in a manner that is a hundred times more severe. He was to overcome not a foe, but his own pride and vanity.

"Thus I said to Godfrey in order to make certain that he had indeed a chivalrous heart, that the amethyst flower was the flower of my life and that I should die if he plucked it. I also told him that if he acquainted anyone with the sacrifice he had made for me, then I should likewise perish, for I had broken the sorceresses' law in asking a favor of him. And Godfrey did master his own pride and vanity. Rather than perform an unchivalrous act he preferred to submit to scorn, disgrace and contempt. He conquered himself. It is the most beautiful victory.

"Take, Godfrey, this flower which you have now verily won and give it to your lady Roxana, as it also is rightfully hers for her brave, trusting and loving heart that has never failed you."

Godfrey accepted, then, the wonderful amethyst flower from the hands of Vivian and presented it to Princess Roxana.

But he did not know that the ring Vivian had given him had a magic power over mountains, as, gentle sirs, you will note in the following tale.

Tale 11

℄ *Upon his return to his own land, he shall drive out the tyrant who shall have seized his throne, and he shall rule long and happily ever after.*

HILE all this was taking place at King Sigmund's court, the land of Prince Gerald groaned under the yoke of cruel tyranny. Gerald cared for nothing but splendid feasts and sumptuous raiment and surrounded himself with such luxury as even the rich royal treasury could not afford. Whereupon he crushed the people with heavy levies, and when not even these would do, he raided the villages of his own subjects, burning and looting them more thoroughly than an enemy would have destroyed them. In addition to these evils—since he permitted no one to oppose his commands or censure them—Gerald dismissed all upright and noble knights and surrounded himself with a pack of wretched minions and flatterers.

His wicked counselors abetted him to ever greater violence and ever fiercer persecution of those who resisted, so that nearly all the knights at the court of Godfrey's father were compelled to hide in the woods, for none of them could be certain of his life or fortune. Moreover, Gerald's counselors entangled him, through senseless and wanton incitement, in a number of wars with his neighbors, bringing suffering and ruin upon the once flourishing country.

Grief-stricken, Roland the Upright, once foremost among the counselors and now a homeless and hounded wanderer, watched the woes and hardships of his country. Finally, an inflexible resolution was born in his heart: even if he had to wander from one end of the world to the other, he must find Prince Godfrey and put an end to the tyrant's rule. Although King Gerald the Cruel had made it known that his nephew Godfrey had perished on a sea voyage, yet in the hearts of the people and knights the hope lived that Godfrey was only hiding to escape persecution by his uncle and that when he reached the age of man he would free his luckless people.

Having formed this bold and noble decision, the venerable Roland left his country disguised as a bard and took to wandering from castle to castle, from land to land, singing of the woes of his people who prayed for the coming of a deliverer. But his pains were futile.

In vain did he cross far-off continents and force his way through forests and across rivers. Nowhere did he come upon the slightest trace of the missing prince.

Despair began to creep into Roland's soul.

Perhaps Gerald had murdered his nephew, and all this search was useless?

But the thought of his hapless country, which Godfrey alone could rescue, sustained the old man and made him wander on. Roland marched farther and farther till he came to the shores of a great sea. There a large merchant ship lay at anchor and the merchants readily consented to take the minstrel on board, that he might beguile with his songs and ballads the long days of their voyage. While at sea Roland learned from them that they carried a cargo of costly carpets, fabrics and jewels for a mighty king, Sigmund the Magnificent.

"He is a great and just monarch," they said, "and in his kingdom all people, husbandmen and merchants alike, enjoy lasting peace, for no enemy would venture to make war upon Godfrey the Conqueror who has no equal among knights."

"Who is this Godfrey the Conqueror?" demanded Roland with curiosity. "Is he a son or kinsman of the king?"

"No," replied the merchants. "Nobody knows his parentage, inasmuch as the king brought him to the court while he was still a boy. It is said that the king found him somewhere in the mountains living among shepherds."

Roland, recalling my predictions, felt his heart throb in his breast and wished his hope and patience might lend wings to the sails.

So it was that as soon as he landed he betook himself forthwith to the royal court.

And when he sang his song before the king and his court, one of the knights suddenly covered his face with the folds of his mantle and wept.

Whereupon Roland the Upright flung away his lute and exclaimed, "You are Godfrey, our beloved prince and lord."

And Godfrey answered, "You are Roland the Upright, my father's friend and adviser."

And weeping they flung themselves into each other's arms, and the entire court and King Sigmund the Magnificent looked on in great amazement. Godfrey then told his story to the king and requested that he be permitted to depart for his own country at once.

The king heard him out and said, "It is right that you should go whither duty calls you. I shall order a hundred vessels rigged out at once to convey you and a host of knights (for I shall give you a thousand of my bravest men) to your native land. We shall await you with impatience, Roxana and I. Return to us victorious as ever."

"Thank you, most gracious lord," replied Godfrey, "but I do not wish to return to my country at the head of foreign cohorts, as might a conqueror. Nor do I wish to contend with my sword for the throne of my father. Here I shall ungird it and leave it. The only weapon I shall take with me to my country will be my fiddle."

"My lord," exclaimed Roland the Upright, "how ill-considered are the words you have uttered. Do you believe that with your music you will move the heart of a tyrant who kills hundreds of people every day? If you do not desire to lead foreign cohorts against your country, then rally your people and your knights. They will all answer your call, arming themselves as best they may."

"I shall call together my people and my knights," said Godfrey, "but I shall have them follow me unarmed. If you are afraid, Roland the Upright, remain here and await my return."

"I will not leave you, my lord, though I know you will lead yourself and your people to certain death and destruction," replied Roland with sorrow.

And King Sigmund and all the knights tried to dissuade Godfrey from carrying out his intention, which they considered folly.

Only Princess Roxana spoke not a word, for she loved Godfrey and had faith in him.

Godfrey, then, took leave of the king and the princess and set off on his long journey.

Scarcely had the news of Godfrey's arrival spread through the country when swarms of people and knights began to collect from everywhere and to welcome him with great jubilation. Godfrey bade them follow him. And he was followed not only by men, but also by half-grown youths, women and children. And since hunger and poverty reigned supreme in the land, their faces were pale and their clothing ragged and shabby.

When I bring these folk before the eyes of my uncle, reflected Godfrey, and show him their misery, his heart will soften. He will recognize that he is unworthy of the crown and will renounce it of his own free will.

But Godfrey did not know the evil heart of that tyrant.

For when the news of his nephew's return reached the court of Gerald the Cruel, he was greatly frightened, but on learning that Godfrey was on his way to the capital at the head of an unarmed crowd of paupers, Gerald was at once reassured, and having assembled his followers he said, "Noble sirs, mount your horses, gird your swords. I shall lead you to a gorgeous festival. We go to pay tribute to my nephew, who proposes to proclaim himself king of ragamuffins and starvelings."

Gerald's toadies burst into laughter and promptly mounted their horses. And Gerald rode in front.

Godfrey, followed by a vast multitude, had just arrived at the road leading to the capital, which ran between the mountains and the sea, when his uncle barred his way.

"Hail, Godfrey," Gerald sneered. "You will not come out of here alive, you or the rebels who have followed you. I have closed in on you from the north and south; to the east you have the sea, and to the west the mountains. I will mow you down to the last man, you audacious riffraff. Nothing can save you, unless

173

the same sea and the mountains come to your rescue."

But scarcely had he uttered these words, noble sirs, scarcely had he uttered these words when something dreadful and horrible, something unheard-of and astounding, occurred.

The waves of the sea began to rise slowly, spraying their silvery foam. First they became terrible billows as in time of storm, then they rose even higher, becoming awesome green mountains whose peaks, capped with white foam, towered sky-high. Then, like a herd of wild steeds with floating snowy manes, they crashed down on Gerald's knights.

A cry of horror burst from a thousand breasts as King Gerald the Cruel and his knights plunged in disorderly flight toward the mountains.

And then, noble sirs, something even more dreadful came to pass.

Gradually and slowly the mountains began to move and with a rumbling that sounded like great claps of thunder they surged forward like an army of giants against Gerald and his knights.

And before the eyes of the horror-stricken people, King Gerald the Cruel and all his host were crushed by the sea and the mountains, thus suffering the penalty for their misdeeds.

No trace was left of them. They might never have existed—save that to this day the road bears the name of "Road of Death."

And this was wrought by those two magic rings which invested Godfrey with dominion over the sea and mountains, whose power Gerald had aroused against himself.

Thus did Prince Godfrey ascend to the throne of his fathers. And the strong no longer dared oppress the weak and everybody could go freely to the royal castle for aid and protection. All the people blessed Godfrey and called him "the Deliverer."

And when order and justice again prevailed in the land, Godfrey, having entrusted the government to Roland the Upright, set out with a great retinue of knights and lords for King Sigmund's castle to fetch his betrothed, Princess Roxana.

Tale 12

⁋ He shall deliver the fairest princess on earth from
the captivity of a ruler who
knocks down mountains at a
single stroke.

HE fairest ladies danced with the handsomest knights, the royal bards sang old songs, and King Sigmund's vassals, the noble dukes, earls and barons, toasted the young, drinking golden mead from tall, gleaming silver cups.

At the king's right sat Prince Godfrey and at his left Princess Roxana, and they conversed about the enchanted garden where they were to dwell, that enchanted garden where thousands of butterflies with rainbow wings dance in the sun.

Just then the guests heard hoofbeats.

At first it was as though a host of knights were speeding posthaste, their hoofs thundering on the road leading to the castle.

"It must be some late guest who is arriving," said the king.

But the clatter grew louder and mightier. Not a hundred, but a thousand horses were thundering on the road.

"Can it be some treacherous foe about to storm the castle by surprise?" whispered the leader of the king's guard, and the knights rose and listened.

179

And the clatter grew louder and mightier. It was no longer the thundering of a thousand horses' hoofs—it was the charging of a hundred thousand wild steeds. Nay, it was deafening thunder roaring, great mountains crashing, it was the whole earth sinking.

The king and all the knights dashed to the ramparts and were struck with terror. On the road leading to the castle galloped a charger as large as the mountain on which the castle stood. The charger seemed hewn from rock, its eyes blazed like two blood-red stars, its nostrils breathed fire, and sparks scattered from under its iron hoofs.

A giant knight, locked from head to toe in black armor, sat the charger, and a flaming plume fluttered from the crest of his helmet.

With a single stroke of his mighty fist mailed in an iron glove, the black knight shattered the fortified gate and flanking towers of the castle, killing a hundred halberdiers. Then he sprang down from his horse and, bending himself in half, entered the great hall where the wedding feast was being held. The royal vassals and courtiers stood spellbound and dared not stir.

Only two people were unaware of the awesome visitor, just as they had been of the din made by the stone horse. Princess Roxana and Prince Godfrey sat holding hands and conversing about the enchanted garden where thousands of butterflies with rainbow wings dance in the sun.

The black knight strode up to the princess and, before she could even utter a cry, he snatched her up in his arms, ran through the door, leaped on his horse and disappeared.

For a while Prince Godfrey stood motionless, pale as a sheet, and then with a fierce cry he pulled his sword clear out of its scabbard, ran from the hall, sprang on his steed and was off in pursuit of the black knight.

"Godfrey, Godfrey," shouted the knights who had meanwhile recovered sufficiently from their terror to grasp what had happened. "Wait, Godfrey! Do not rush after that giant, for he will kill you at one stroke. Wait, let us consult together and plan what we are to do. Godfrey, Godfrey!"

But Prince Godfrey did not hear. Helmetless, with uplifted sword, he charged at top speed after the black knight, shouting, "Halt, halt, vile dastard! Halt and face me in combat."

But the black knight did not so much as look back. Or perhaps Godfrey's voice did not reach him, for the hoofbeats of his horse drowned out every sound. These hoofs made such huge holes in the ground that Godfrey's horse could hardly leap over them. The black knight moved farther and farther away and soon Godfrey lost sight of him.

Then Prince Godfrey, he who was called "the Conqueror" and "the Indomitable" wept like a child. His knight's heart could not bear to think of his betrothed, golden-haired Princess Roxana, dainty as a flower or as a butterfly, in the hands of the black brigand, and that he, Godfrey, could not save her.

But it would be unworthy of a true knight to despair when all was not yet lost. So Godfrey stifled his anguish and sped onward in pursuit of the stone horse.

He rode for two days and two nights, without food or drink, and on the third day he came to a huge mountain. Here he saw that the tracks of the stone horse had disappeared as if both mount and rider had sunk into the ground. But Godfrey did not lose hope.

Such a horse could indeed hurdle mountains, and its hoofprints were surely to be found on the other side. With this in mind, Godfrey alighted from his horse and leading it by the bridle began to climb the steep upward path. Boulders rolled away from under his feet; hunger and thirst plagued him; the heavy armor, which he had not taken off for three days, cramped him and tore into his flesh. But not for nothing was Godfrey called "the Indomitable." He marched steadfastly on and on.

Meanwhile the early winter night had fallen and a storm had buried all the mountain paths in snow.

Now Godfrey knew not whither to go. As he looked about he heard a gentle groan, and saw a little doe lying at his feet gazing up at him wistfully with its large black eyes.

Godfrey bent and stroked its pretty head.

"What is wrong with you, poor thing?" he said sympathetically. "What a pity that you cannot speak. At any rate, I cannot let you freeze to death in the snow." And removing his mantle, Godfrey covered the doe.

But the doe sprang up and said gaily:

"You are wrong, Prince Godfrey, you are wrong.

Tonight is Christmas Eve and on this wonderful night all animals can speak in memory of our Lord Jesus, who was born in their midst."

"But how do you know my name?" asked Godfrey, surprised.

"She who sent me to you said to me, 'You will know him because he is the handsomest knight.' 'There are many handsome knights,' I answered. 'Then you will know him because he is the bravest,' she said. 'How shall I see that?' 'You will know him, then, by observing that even though he himself may be in distress he will not pass indifferently the suffering of another.' And thus I knew you. Hail to you, Prince Godfrey."

"And who is it that sent you to me?" inquired Godfrey.

"Your betrothed, Princess Roxana," replied the doe.

"Indeed? Then you saw her? Did you speak to her? Do you know where she is? Can you lead me to her?"

"No, Godfrey. I cannot do this. Your betrothed is a prisoner of the King of Gales and Darkness, of Glaciers and Abysses. Certain death awaits any brave knight who would dare to defy him. Roxana entreats you not to search for her or you will perish."

"I will perish or I will free her," exclaimed Godfrey, drawing his sword. "Lead me to where she is."

The little doe shook its head.

"I cannot do this, Godfrey. But follow me and I will lead you to the hut of an old hermit. He knows not only all the paths in the mountains, but also ways of coping with the King of Darkness and he can give you much good advice."

"Very well, my little doe," said Godfrey. "Lead me to him, lead me quickly, for my heart burns with impatience."

They descended, then, into a small valley. In the bright moonlight Godfrey sighted the hermit's hut. The hermit, an old man whose hair was as white as a dove, sat on the doorstep, gazing into the distance as if waiting for someone.

"Welcome, young knight," he said on seeing Godfrey before him. "It is good that you happened by, because I am so old that I am no longer strong enough to chop wood, and surely you will not refuse me this favor. The hatchet is inside."

Godfrey was in a great hurry, but it was ill-becoming for a knight to deny help to one who was weaker than himself. So he bowed silently to the old man, took the hatchet and went to work.

"There, you see what youth and brawn can do," said the hermit after a while. "In less time than it takes to say the Lord's Prayer, I have been supplied with enough firewood to last all winter. Go inside and lay a fire in the hearth."

Godfrey was in a great hurry, but it ill became a knight to deny help to one who was weaker than himself. And he stepped inside the hut and kindled a fire.

"And now," said the hermit, "go down into the cellar. You will find there a jug of wine and a loaf of wheat bread. Put the jug near the fire and when the wine is warm come back here with the bread and the warmed wine."

Godfrey burned with impatience, but it was ill-becoming for a knight to deny help to one who was weaker than himself, and so he again complied with the hermit's demand.

"Thank you, my son," said the hermit. "Now sit here by my side and restore yourself with bread and wine, for you have eaten nothing for three days and a strenuous time lies ahead of you."

"How do you know?" exclaimed the amazed knight.

The hermit smiled.

"I read in the stars," he responded. "Raise your head. The entire sky that you see there is to me a large open book where the fate of the world is set down in silver letters on dark sapphire pages. I knew you would come here even before you had thought of it. Listen, then, to my advice. Do you see that wall of ice looming opposite us, the summit buried in the clouds?"

"I do," said Godfrey.

"You must climb up to that summit and then jump into the dark abyss that you will see there."

"Very well," replied Godfrey, as calmly as if the hermit had advised him to walk down the carpeted stairs leading to a ballroom. "And then?"

"Then you will find yourself in a large hall, the walls of which will be formed by four mountains. In the center of the hall you will see your enemy seated on a granite throne. He will attempt to awe you with his might. Whatever he will do then, you must do the same, even if it seems beyond the power of man.

187

If you will do all this with faith in yourself you will surely succeed, for tonight is the miraculous Christmas night when evil cannot triumph over good."

"Thank you," said Godfrey, rising, "thank you for your hospitality and for your advice. Will you permit me to leave my horse here, as I cannot climb on ice if I take him with me?"

"Leave him," replied the hermit. "God speed your safe return. Take along this hatchet with which you chopped my wood; it may serve you in good stead."

Godfrey bowed, thanked the hermit once more for everything and was on his way. Walking briskly, he soon reached the foot of the icy cliff. But in vain did he go around it looking for the slightest niche, for the slightest foothold that would permit him to climb up. The cliff was steep and smooth as a mirror. Surely none but a bird could get to the top. Godfrey was seized with despair. Should he go away and leave Roxana at the mercy of the loathsome brigand? Should he let her die pining for the sun at the bottom of the dark abyss? No, never. If he could not climb up that cliff, he would break it down.

And taking the hatchet, he swung it with all his might into the wall of ice. And then something extraordinary happened: the hatchet broke loose from his hand and began to run up the cliff, hacking steps therein as it went.

Godfrey raised his eyes skyward, wishing to thank God for the miracle of the aid thus afforded to him. Just above his head he perceived a star gleaming with such wonderful brilliance that it outshone all others in beauty.

Godfrey then knew in his heart that this was the Christmas Star, and he began to climb upward, full of joy and great encouragement.

It was truly no easy climbing.

An icy wind blew at him from the wall, his hands froze fast to the icy steps, and any slip would mean death. But the Christmas Star was overhead, and Godfrey's heart was brimming with great love, so he felt neither cold nor pain nor fear.

At length he arrived at the top. Below him gaped a bottomless chasm. When he looked down into it Godfrey trembled for the first time in his life. Dead silence and darkness reigned there. A stone which he sent to the bottom with his foot fell without making a sound. The smell of mold and rot enveloped him.

Godfrey wavered . . .

But instantly he recalled that down there, in that bottomless depth, he would find Roxana, and stretching out his arms he plunged into the abyss.

For a few seconds he fell into the darkness at lightning speed then suddenly he felt that someone's powerful arm clasped him, breaking his fall, and sat him down on the ground.

Godfrey found himself, as the hermit had foretold, in a large hall whose walls were formed by four mountains. In the center rose a throne of huge granite rocks and upon it sat the King of Darkness and Abysses.

"Where have you come from, human ant, and how dare you enter my castle?" he demanded wrathfully. His voice was like the roar of thunder, and it was echoed three times by the walls.

"I have come to deliver Roxana and to punish you, vile brigand, for having dared to imprison her," retorted Godfrey proudly, and he himself was surprised at the might of his voice, for it sounded like a bell of bronze and was echoed six times by the walls. The King of Darkness laughed out with a hideous howl, such as could make the bravest knight shudder.

"Wretched fool," he shouted. "You mean to set

yourself against my will? Roxana will become my wife even if she resists more than she does now and even if she is defended by a hundred knights such as you, all of whom I can fell with one puff."

And he puffed. And his breath was such that it lifted Godfrey like a feather and hurled him to the ground.

Godfrey got up, calling out, "If you are so strong, then I who fight for Roxana ought to be even stronger."

And without stopping to think that the giant whom he meant to engage commanded all the hurricanes, he puffed with the whole might of his lungs.

Dear heaven, what a gale ensued. Not only was the black knight hurled to the ground but his granite throne was overturned and shattered to bits.

Before Godfrey had time to recover from his surprise at the sight of what he had done, the King of Darkness got up and spoke thus:

"I see that you are stronger than I had thought, or perhaps you are assisted by some powers unknown to me. Do not think, however, that you are stronger than I. Look what I can do."

And approaching one of the walls, he pushed it

with all his might. The mountain trembled on its foundations and tumbled down with a frightening crash.

"And now what?" asked the King of Darkness with a sneer. "And now, Roxana's knight, can you do the same?"

Godfrey seethed with anger, and without stopping to think whether it was within the power of man to uproot mountains, he approached another wall and straining his strength to the utmost, he pushed it.

An even more frightful crash was heard as not only that wall but also the two others came down, crashing apart.

"I see," said the King of Darkness gloomily, "that you are stronger than I. You must be the Knight of the Star of the Nativity and tonight no one can overcome you. I am going away from here so as not to perish by your hand. But do not think that you have freed Roxana. I am casting a spell on her and on you. From now on you shall be invisible to each other. In vain will you search for her in my hundred chambers till daybreak. And when morning comes and the Christmas Star is extinguished, I will return

192

here to deal with you. But at that time you will no longer be able to uproot mountains; this night alone belongs to you."

And with these words, the King of Darkness departed and Godfrey was left alone. For a moment he paid no attention to the words of the sorcerer. Proud and happy at the defeat of his foe, he went from one chamber to another in search of Roxana.

But the dark, immense and dismal halls were empty and silent. Godfrey's spurs rang out on the stone floor, and the adjoining rooms sent back a dull echo of his steps, an echo that was strangely frightening in the silence.

An odd feeling took hold of Godfrey. It was not fear, but a sense of menacing solitude. Though the halls were empty, danger seemed to lurk behind each of the huge, rugged granite columns which supported the stone walls.

Godfrey drew his sword and walked on, the bared sword in his hand, calling: "Roxana, Roxana!"

Suddenly he heard her voice trembling with happiness:

"Godfrey, is it you? Godfrey, Godfrey!"

"Where are you, Roxana?" he called, running into the hall whence the voice came. "Roxana, where are you?"

"I am here, Godfrey. But where are you? I hear you, but I cannot see you. Godfrey, Godfrey!"

"Here I am, Roxana. But I cannot see you in the dark. Here I am, Roxana. But where are you? Roxana, Roxana!"

They ran, now moving away from each other, now coming closer, straying through ever new halls and passageways, now ceasing to hear each other, now hearing each other again, so close they seemed almost within each other's reach. Meanwhile, their voices echoed over and over: "Roxana," "Godfrey," "Roxana," "Godfrey," "Roxana."

All in vain, however. The spell cast upon them by the King of Darkness held.

At length they came into the room where Godfrey had been at grips with the black knight. It had no vault, above it the starry sky glittered with a thousand lights. Godfrey knelt down, and raising his eyes to the Christmas Star which gleamed with wonderful brilliance, he began to pray.

"O Lord who guided me as a child across the sea

on the wings of birds: O Lord who gave power to the arm of a lad when my knightly honor was about to be assailed: O Lord who hast given me more than power, more than glory, who hast given me Roxana, do not suffer this evil sorcerer to triumph over me. And if I have been at fault and you wish to punish me, then punish me alone and I implore you to preserve Roxana."

And while Godfrey the Conqueror was praying he suddenly felt that someone touched his arm.

He looked around and saw the little doe which he had covered with his mantle lest it should die in the snow. The doe had now brought Godfrey his mantle, and handing it to him, said, "Cover yourself with it, Godfrey. It has acquired magic power through your deed."

Godfrey threw the mantle over his shoulders and at that very moment he heard Roxana's joyous cry.

"There you are, Godfrey. I see you."

And he felt her arms around his neck. He covered her with his mantle and then her golden head was on his breast. He seized her in his arms and together they sped toward the hermit's hut, running as fast as they could.

hen the stars disappeared and day broke, Godfrey and Roxana were far away from the kingdom of darkness and abysses.

Together they rode on a white road through a white forest and Godfrey held Roxana on his saddle in front of him, and they conversed about the enchanted garden, that enchanted garden where thousands of rainbow-winged butterflies dance in the sun. And the forest was white and still, like a bride on her wedding day. And the icicles glittered in the sun like diamonds. And a silvery radiance seemed to be reflected from the snow.

But deep in the forest dwelt forty fearsome bandits, who robbed travelers on the roads. Their leader, called the chieftain, having spied among the trees Godfrey's glittering golden armor and Princess Roxana's shining golden hair, called his henchmen together and said, "The armor of that knight shall be your booty, and that lovely wench whom he holds on the saddle in front of him shall be mine."

So they took their maces and hatchets and knives and spears and ugly-looking swords, and shouting they set upon Godfrey from all sides.

196

Ho, what a pity that you were not there! What a pity you did not see how Godfrey the Conqueror contended with forty robbers in that forest.

His sword came down like lightning on their necks and splinters flew from their maces under his blows.

Ho, what a pity you were not there! What a pity that you did not see how forty robbers fled from one knight.

When they were left alone, Princess Roxana inquired of Godfrey, "Are you wounded, Godfrey?"

"No," replied Godfrey, "I am not wounded, Roxana."

But he did not speak the truth, for his heart was bleeding beneath his golden armor, but he did not wish to frighten away the smile from the lips of his beloved.

They rode on, then, and Godfrey held Roxana in front of him on the saddle, and they conversed about the enchanted garden, that enchanted garden where thousands of rainbow-winged butterflies dance in the sun.

Meanwhile King Sigmund had summoned all his vassals and proclaimed that to him who would free

Princess Roxana from the power of the black knight would be given half the kingdom and the princess herself for a wife.

Now, among King Sigmund's vassals there was an earl by the name of Rodrigo. He was said to assault travelers who chanced through his forests, to rob widows and orphans of their possessions, and to disregard the laws of knights in combat. The king himself had several times summoned him to trial, but somehow Rodrigo had always contrived to elude punishment. Earl Rodrigo now gathered his troops and spoke thus:

"I myself will not go in search of the black knight, for only a fool will court disaster, but I shall lie in ambush with you by the road leading to the castle, and if that madman Godfrey has succeeded in delivering the princess, we will wrest her from him and slay him, or else wring from him a pledge on his honor as a knight that he will keep silent. Then we will bring Roxana to the king saying we have freed her from captivity, and we shall receive the reward, and win great fame besides."

Ah, that Rodrigo was no knight, but a veritable brigand.

Thus, just as Godfrey and Roxana arrived almost in sight of the towers of the royal castle, Rodrigo and his band set upon them with drawn swords.

Prince Godfrey, exceedingly surprised, said, "Earl Rodrigo, and you gallant knights, has madness so completely possessed you that you cannot tell friend from foe? Do you not know the daughter of your king, and myself, her future husband, your companion in so many raids?"

Thus spoke Godfrey the Conqueror without drawing his sword, for his noble heart suspected no treason.

"Not you," retorted Rodrigo, "but I will become Roxana's husband. If you surrender her of your free will, and swear that you will vouch before the king that it was I who set her free, then I will spare your life. If you will not do this, you shall perish miserably. We are one hundred and twenty."

Godfrey went pale with anger and indignation, and drawing his sword he rushed at Rodrigo with a cry: "Perish, you knave."

And this villain, a disgrace to all the knights, would have perished under that mighty blow had he not saved himself by adroitly evading it.

Thereupon Rodrigo's band fell upon Godfrey from all sides.

No, no longer can our youth execute such giddy flourishes, such cross strokes, such masterly thrusts with the lance, and, above all, no longer can he stand up to his foes, whatever their number, in such stanch and unyielding fashion, and rather perish than disgrace himself.

Ho, 'tis a pity that you were not there. 'Tis a pity that you did not see Godfrey breast that onrush. Not many minutes had passed before Godfrey unhorsed seven and twenty knights.

But Godfrey was wounded and his sword clanged more and more weakly against the armor of his enemies. He was only one in combat against overwhelming odds. Attacking him from behind, they dragged him from the saddle, bound him with ropes and threw him to the ground.

Ho, 'twas no chivalrous combat.

Earl Rodrigo stood before his fettered opponent and taunted him thus:

"Where is your pride, Godfrey? What has become of your fame as a knight? There you lie at my feet and your life is at my mercy. And yet they called you 'the

Conqueror,' Godfrey. And yet they called you 'the Conqueror!'"

And he rested the point of his sword on Godfrey's breast.

Without turning pale or winking an eye, Godfrey replied, looking steadily into his enemy's face:

"Here I lie at your feet and my life is at your mercy, and yet, nonetheless, I am Godfrey the Conqueror, while you are a contemptible and vile rogue."

Rodrigo shook with rage and would have thrust his sword into the knight's breast, had not Princess Roxana stayed his hand.

"Insolent fool," she exclaimed. "Do you believe that after murdering Godfrey you will be able to force me into silence by pleas or by threats? Truly, it would avail you better if you freed Godfrey and threw yourself on his mercy, for I know that he is a forgiving man. If you will not do this, the headman shall, by the king's command, unfasten your spurs, the headman shall break your sword, and your head shall roll under the headman's ax."

Rodrigo burst into frightful laughter.

"It is truly well, Roxana, that you have shown yourself to be not a fainthearted dove but an eagle. I will have your tongue torn out and shall tell the king that it is the black knight who maimed you thus. You shall keep silent, Roxana, I swear by my sword, you shall keep silent."

"You are mistaken, Rodrigo, you are mistaken. My father will look into my eyes and in my eyes he will read the whole truth. I will tell him everything with my eyes."

"I shall order these eyes burned out, these eyes which Godfrey has likened in his songs to mountain lakes, and I shall say that it is the black knight who maimed you thus. You shall keep silent, Roxana, I swear by my sword, you shall keep silent."

"You are mistaken, Rodrigo, you are mistaken. I shall wring my hands, I shall tear out my hair and shall tell all to my father."

"I shall cut off your golden hair, of which Godfrey sang that it is a harp's strings. I shall chop off your white hands, which Godfrey said are like lilies. You shall keep silent Roxana, I swear by my sword, you shall keep silent."

Godfrey trembled, for he knew that those were not empty threats and that this villain was capable of any outrage.

"Do not heed her words, Rodrigo," he said. "What does her raving matter? For she is mad with despair. Kill me, but do not touch her."

"No!" exclaimed Roxana. "Better to kill me and take him to the castle. Tell my father that the King of Darkness hurled me into the abyss, that Godfrey went mad with anguish, and you had great difficulty in saving him. My father will then disbelieve his words and you will receive half the kingdom as a reward, for he loves Godfrey like a son."

"No, rather kill me, Rodrigo."

"No, rather me."

While they thus wrangled over which of them was to die, Rodrigo's knights suddenly became aware that a queer thing was happening to them.

They felt that something clutched their throats, that something burned their eyelids and filled their eyes with moisture. And none ventured to raise his eyes toward the other, and each one sought to hide his face in the folds of his cloak.

These men, who had long since turned from knights to brigands, suddenly felt repentance and shame for having trampled upon their own honor as knights and for permitting a felon to lead them to crime.

And suddenly one of them named Rudolf, stepping forth from their midst, shouted, "Will you allow this most valiant and most celebrated of knights and this lady of matchless beauty to perish? Will you cover yourselves with shame by mistreating a prisoner and a lady?"

Whereupon the band replied as one man: "No. Certainly not."

And as they were very obdurate and scarcely charitable men, one of them added presently:

"And would it not be better if we tore out that wretched rascal's tongue, if we burned out his eyes and then hung him from a tree by the road, since it is not fitting for him to die in another way?"

And once more the entire troop replied as one man, "It would be better indeed."

Rodrigo's eyes wandered over his men, and seeing their stern faces he shook like an aspen leaf and fled. But before long he was seized by a dozen hands and was brought before Godfrey, whose bonds were just then being cut.

Rodrigo fell on his knees before Godfrey and implored mercy, embracing Godfrey's legs, for I warrant you that he who abuses the weak grovels before the strong, and he who is brave against the defense-less is a coward when facing the armed.

Godfrey glanced at him pityingly and said:

"It is not for a knight to ply the headman's trade. Turn him loose."

However, one of the band ventured: "How can it be that he should go unpunished?"

Godfrey replied, "What greater punishment do you demand for him, since he has already suffered the greatest one?"

The knights, greatly surprised, inquired, "Which one?"

And Godfrey answered, "Dishonor." And he fainted, for he was bleeding from his wounds.

Princess Roxana rushed up to him, and laying his head on her knees she began to unfasten his armor. The knights surrounded them in a circle and each of them offered her what he could—linen, water, or wine.

And when Godfrey had drunk a cup of wine, he regained his strength completely.

He mounted his horse, seating Roxana before him on the saddle, and commanded the knights to start on their way, dispatching one of them ahead as a messenger. This messenger, then, rode at top speed to the capital to announce to King Sigmund that Roxana had been freed, and his eyes nearly popped out at the sight of the wonders that he beheld on his way.

The sun shone as warmly as if it were May and not December. The snow melted. Anemones, violets, marsh-marigolds and daisies bloomed in the meadows. There were green buds everywhere on the branches of trees. Birds twittered on their way back from overseas, and cherry orchards were in full bloom in the villages by the roads.

So that knight plucked a few flower-laden branches, and tapping them on the windows of the village huts, he called:

"Prince Godfrey and Princess Roxana are coming back. Prince Godfrey and Princess Roxana are returning."

All who could move jumped up, and picking flowers on their way they ran to meet Roxana and Godfrey.

And so it was that Godfrey and Roxana rode on a flower-strewn road amid the joyous cheers of the people.

And birds flew above them, singing lustily and tirelessly.

And children ran before them, holding sprays of blossom-covered cherry and apple branches in their hands.

And Godfrey held Roxana before him in the saddle, and they conversed about the enchanted garden, that enchanted garden where thousands of rainbow-winged butterflies dance in the sun.

And when they rode into the capital, the bells of all the churches rang their greetings, and hundreds of colored flags waved to them from all windows, and knights wearing golden armor saluted them, dipping their swords before them.

That same evening a great banquet was held in the castle. The fairest ladies danced with the handsomest knights, the royal troubadours sang old lays, and King Sigmund's vassals, the noble dukes, earls and barons, toasted the young couple by drinking golden mead from silver cups.

And Prince Godfrey and Princess Roxana?

Prince Godfrey and Princess Roxana strolled about their enchanted garden, where blood-purple roses and lily-white orchids flourished, and they watched as thousands of butterflies, thousands of rainbow-winged butterflies, danced in the sun.